Among the Willows
and Other Strange Tales

I0552411

ISBN 978-1-7333177-5-7

Written by John Opalenik
Cover art by Amanda Opalenik
Edited by Nancy Manning

Printed in The United States of America

opalenikj@gmail.com
Visit www.johnopalenik.com

Dedicated to my wife, Amanda. In eternal gratitude for everything you are, everything you do, and everything you create.

That Dog Won't Hunt

Dallas Weaver sat in the painted rocking chair that creaked as much as his old bones. He sipped a glass of whiskey more slowly than he'd have done in his youth. After nearly four decades as sheriff of Coyote Bluffs, Texas, he'd outgrown the need to prove himself that had been such a driving force in his first years as a lawman. The whiskey didn't burn like it used to and that was alright as far as he was concerned. Dallas Weaver had burned plenty over the years and he didn't yearn for the fire like the young man next to him did.

The rocking chair that sat six feet to Weaver's left creaked, but with the groans of not having been fully broken in yet. It wasn't a new chair by any means, but it didn't have the same kind of mileage that Weaver's did. This seat was occupied by Manuel Montoya, a young lawman born in Mexico who'd come up to Texas as a boy. He'd been a soldier fighting for the union and had made a name for himself fighting at the Battle of Palmito Ranch up in Cameron County back in '65. He'd been a promising deputy in the ten years following. The only problem was that the sheriff he was working under up in Encino wasn't set to retire for at least another ten years, and Manuel wasn't set to wait that long to become sheriff himself. He was fond of telling those he'd met that "Montoya" meant mountain and that's how he saw himself, an immovable object between the good people of the West and those who would bring violence and depravity to the townships and camps kept the chaos of the wilds at bay. He burned. Burned with a passion to prove himself, to become a lawman of legend. Montoya always kept his clothing clean and his guns well oiled, but he always left stubble on his chin. He always thought the clean shaven look made him look younger than he was and that wasn't what he wanted the world to see.

He downed his whiskey in two quick gulps and stifled the cough that it had caused. "You held onto this township for a long time."

"I did." Weaver nodded as he thought back on the decades of serving the township. Coyote Bluffs was a fine township and he liked to think that his life's work had something to do with that.

"What was it like when you took up the post?" He leaned forward, in awe of the sheriff but at the same time trying to present himself as a worthy successor.

"Wasn't much more than a camp. More folks lived in tents than in proper houses. Coyote Bluffs was just a few dozen prospectors panning for gold in the runoff of the Colorado River and other folks looking to make their livings off the fortunes and misfortunes of them that panned in the creek."

Montoya smiled with a nostalgia for a time he never knew. "Must've been wild."

"Being a lawman when there ain't no law leaves more room for whatever you got lingering in the back rooms of your soul to creep out into the world. I seen lawmen in camps with no law become the finest example of morality and virtue...of course, just as often they turn into monsters twice as evil as whatever shitheel they claimed they was there to stop. Folks like that never last though. Either the town gets too civilized for them to get away with it and they move on, or the place stays wild and the chaos they'd helped build sorts them out." Weaver took a short gulp of his whiskey and sighed. "Aw Hell...I'm rambling. What was it you were asking me?"

"I asked you where you got that scar." Montoya drew his finger across the top of his own right eyebrow, mirroring where a groove had been cut into Weaver's a lifetime ago.

"Oh that ain't nothing." Weaver waved his hand. "Some lucky son of a bitch took a shot at me before I put him away to hang the next morning. Funny thing is, he disappeared from his cell that night. Never found out how he got out, but he never raised any hell around these parts again, and I suppose that's what matters most." Weaver sat up in his chair, suddenly more aware than he'd been a moment before. "That wasn't it. You asked me about the biggest trouble to ever come to these parts, or something to that effect."

Montoya wasn't sure that he'd even asked a question like that, but it had certainly been on his mind. He didn't want to pry, but since his heart burned with a yearning for the lifetime of tales within the man he sat next to, he made one up. "When was the first time you saved Coyote Bluffs? I mean really saved it. The first time it was just you standing between civilization and the wilds."

"When you put it like that, I can only think of one time." His expression grew more serious in a way that made him feel every year that he'd lived and reminded him of every scar he'd earned over the course of his life. "It was strange times being a lawman in a place that doesn't technically have laws. Hell, nobody even made me the sheriff. It was just agreed upon by the folks around town since I was a lawman back East." Weaver looked off into the distance as if the vast horizon of the desert held visions of his past. "More chaos, but the simpler kind. Things didn't get complicated until Boyd Turla struck rich back in '39.

The gold brought people and business and greed. The greed is what left an opening."

Montoya hesitated to correct Weaver, but wanted to show that he'd done his reading on the town he'd soon be guardian of. "I thought what put Coyote Bluffs on the map was when Theodore Watkins struck big back in 1840."

"It certainly did." Weaver tipped his hat to Montoya, acknowledging respect for what he'd learned and his worth as a new lawman. "Watkins was the first one to fall victim to the greed, but that was after Boyd unearthed something he shouldn't have."

Montoya considered what sounded to him like a prelude. "In my experience, money and women are the two reasons a man will commit a crime, but that don't mean we were meant to leave the gold in the ground."

"Not all gold is the same." Weaver's expression grew more serious. "And this was one fortune that would have been better off unclaimed."

Manuel Montoya didn't say anything, sensing that Weaver didn't need any more prompting for him to tell the story of the one time he'd felt he'd saved the township.

"It started out small...it always does. Boyd Turla was just your average prospector, out here on his own, no family to speak of, but with big plans. He thought that panning for gold would give him a small fortune that he could then turn into a profitable business, I don't know what kind. Hell. I don't even think he did. He just figured that if he had enough money to get something going, he could do it."

"You want another?" Manuel held up his empty glass.

"I'm fine. Thanks." Weaver waved a hand, gesturing for Manuel to forego another drink and return to the porch.

Montoya sat back down, the thirst for knowledge greater than for drink. "What happened when Boyd found his claim?"

"He kept it half-hidden."

"What do you mean?"

"Boyd didn't try to conceal that he'd struck rich, but he kept the location of his find to himself," Weaver chuckled to himself at the memory of Boyd's boyish reaction to becoming a rich man. "First thing he did was head into the saloon and buy a round for everyone who was there. When he came up dead the next morning, nobody was surprised. What surprised everyone was that he still had plenty of gold on him when an old Arlo, another prospector, found him."

"He got killed for striking it rich, and the one who did it didn't even rob him?" Manuel's mouth puckered as if he'd tasted something foul. "That ain't normal."

"I tried not to let that cloud my mind when I was figuring out what exactly happened. There were plenty of reasons the killer couldn't have completed the robbery, but I didn't want to pigeonhole myself into thinking one way about it until I knew more. The next thing that struck me as odd when I started asking around was that nobody seemed to hear the shot."

"Did they do him in with a purse gun?" Manuel suggested. "Sometimes they don't make much of a sound compared to other guns."

"The thought crossed my mind, but the hole left in him looked like it'd come from a rifle, and unless he spun on his way down, the shot seemed like it'd come from out of town in the desert." Weaver explained. "I took my horse out that way and from up on the ridge, I saw one man with a rifle and a prairie antelope corpse at his feet."

"You mean to tell me it was just a stray shot that killed Boyd?" Montoya looked to Weaver doubtfully.

"I'm going to be saying this a lot over the course of this story, but it ain't that simple." Weaver took a deep breath, fully aware that once he started telling this part of his experience, he'd have to tell the whole thing. "I got down from the ridge and found the hunter, a man by the name of Moss. When I found him, I complimented him on his kill and asked if he'd taken shots at any other antelope before dawn. That's when he started to hesitate. 'I don't want no trouble.' He says. 'I'd never raise up my rifle unless it's to hunt or to defend myself.' I was more than a little suspicious after hearing an answer like that, so I asked him if he'd taken another shot that night."

Montoya leaned forward, as if Weaver were going to whisper what happened next.

"He started off by telling me he didn't hit anything, but that he saw what he thought was a black wolf near the spot where he'd made camp, but when he fired at it, mostly just to scare it off, the thing stood up and took the shape of a man."

"You've got to be shitting me. Sounds like he damn near blew a man's head off when he was squatting down to take a shit in the woods," Manuel joked. Normally he wouldn't be so casual about someone behaving so recklessly, but since he already knew that nobody got hit, he allowed himself to see the humor in it.

"I thought the same thing at first, but when he ran up to see if the man was okay, there wasn't anybody there," Dallas explained. "I got him to show me the spot where he'd fired the shot and sure enough, it was a straight shot from there to where Boyd Turla's body was found. Of course I couldn't haul him in for that. You couldn't make a shot from that far away if you tried, and here in Coyote Bluffs we aren't in the business of looking for crimes where there aren't any to be found. It was ruled as an accidental death and aside from Moss talking about that wolf turning into a man every time you got a couple drinks in him, most folks didn't think about it anymore. Most folks were more concerned with where Boyd had struck rich. He never told anybody the location, but he did say that there was too much gold for him to carry at his find. That got the prospectors talking, and the rumors spread around the township like wildfire. It wasn't long before men from all walks of life were venturing out into the creeks and the land where the forest met the desert where Boyd was known to dig."

"I can see how that would lead to more crime in town, but how did it end up in a situation where you had to really save the town?" Montoya asked, hoping that the story wasn't just about something so routine as folks fighting over gold in a mining camp.

"Most folks went out searching during the day. Makes sense that if you're looking for something, you'd do so when you've got daylight on your side." Dallas paused. "But not Watkins. He went out in the dead of night."

"Sounds like he knew something that the rest of the people searching didn't," Manuel offered.

"I don't know if you'd say he knew something...more that he had a feeling," Weaver continued. "Now what I'm about to tell you may sound crazy. That's what I thought when I first heard it, since I wasn't there for it. But when I stack it up next to what had come after that I'd seen with my own two eyes, it makes sense...as far as things like these can make sense." Dallas Weaver paused, considering how to preface the sharp turn his tale was about to take. "Tell me, Montoya. Do you believe in evil?"

He thought about it as more than a simple question, but more of a probe into his deepest held beliefs. "I don't think that a man can fight in a war, then go on to be a lawman, seeing what we see, and not believe in evil."

"Good. Because from what I've been able to piece together, what Watkins found out there was evil on four legs. In that natural borderland where the desert stopped and the forest began, a wolf came to him, bigger than any wolf you've ever seen and blacker than the darkness it emerged from. When it spoke to him, it didn't speak like you or I would. The words just appeared in his mind and hit him like a punch in the gut, just by looking in its eyes."

Montoya found this a little hard to believe, but the respect that he felt for Weaver after three days of patrolling Coyote Bluffs with him gave Manuel the patience to hear him out. He'd seen some strange things in his days fighting in the Union Army like the time he saw his friend Bill Hudson get fired at by a Confederate officer's revolver six times at point blank range and the officer missed every single shot, or the time he saw he could've sworn he saw an apparition of Captain Reese, his commanding officer two days after he'd been killed in battle. He figured there was much more to this world than the things folks see every day, so he gave Weaver a chance.

"The thing told him where to look for Boyd's gold find, and told him that he'd only keep it for as long as Boyd did if he didn't agree to certain terms."

Montoya leaned forward, entranced. "What were the terms?"

"Nothing that didn't serve Watkins' own interests," Weaver mused. "He had to agree that he'd secure the gold find, and use his newfound wealth to establish himself as a prominent player in Coyote Bluffs and never to reveal how he'd found the gold."

"If he agreed never to tell, then how do you know about it?"

"I didn't for a time. Nobody did," Weaver explained. "All we knew was that within a week, Theodore Watkins was a rich man. He had everything that any of the rich folks in the cities back East had, save for the family history to back up his wealth."

"What happened next?"

"The same thing that happens whenever a town becomes a rich place. More people came with hope in their eyes. Businessmen came to bring vice to the town, hoping that those who struck rich would spend the gold they'd found on gambling, whiskey, and women, and despite the fact that they ran games of chance, their plan was a more sure thing. A prospector may or may not find anything on a given day in the creek, but as long as there was gold to spend, there were people willing to spend it," Sheriff Weaver explained. "Things in town began to move at a faster pace in those days. Folks coming into fortunes, losing it just as quickly, and if you throw a bunch of men who are mad, drunk, and armed into a saloon, it's only a matter of time."

"Like I said, nobody knew about the deal Theodore Watkins struck in the woods. People around here, myself included, just figured it was the natural progression. A camp becomes a township, and if there's money to be made, it becomes a city. It would only be a matter of time until the railroad came through."

"But it never did." Manuel gestured to the town that lay beyond Sheriff Weaver's front porch, which was further developed than it was in 1840, but barely showed the remnants of the wild place that Weaver had been describing. Only one saloon remained on the corner, and while there was a nightly poker game, these weren't the kind of games of chance that ended in frequent shoot-outs.

"No." Sheriff Weaver smiled and took a slow sip from his glass. "It didn't turn out that way." Weaver stopped talking to tip his hat to a few ladies who walked by with their husbands, likely on their way back from church. "Like I said, the town got rich and it was no secret that it was all because of Theodore Watkins and his gold claim. By the time spring came, half the other prospectors stopped working their own meager claims and started working for him. He was happy to be a big shot at first, but after a few months with that kind of money and that kind of power under his control, he started to see what kind of man he really was."

"Reminds me of something my father used to say," Manuel replied. "He said that a man shows his true colors when he's on top. When he's under somebody's thumb, you only see who he knows he's got to be to survive."

"Sounds like a man with some wisdom to him."

Manuel shrugged his shoulders. "Sometimes."

Sheriff Weaver thought about his own father and how, like Manuel said, was always under the thumb of someone with power, and so rarely got to show the world who he really was. "After seeing men who worked for him kill workers in his name, Theodore Watkins knew he wasn't cut out to be the next gold tycoon, and so he started to make nightly pilgrimages out to the woods to speak to the wolf, begging it to take back everything it had led him to find. But he came to find that corruption is like whiskey. It's easy enough to pour out, but good luck getting it back into the bottle."

"Speaking of which…" Manuel trailed off as he stood up to go inside and fill his glass.

"Hold off on that, Montoya." Sheriff Weaver raised his hand, gently gesturing for the young man to stop. "I want to walk the length of the thoroughfare, let the folks know that we're looking after them as they go about their mid-day business. Best we do that without whiskey on our breath."

"Aren't you going to tell me how things turned out with Watkins and the wolf first?" Manuel protested.

"It'll wait until after we see to the township." Weaver stood up from his chair, and although his bones creaked with age, standing up to patrol the town he'd sworn to protect filled him with an energy that transcended age. "I'll finish up telling you over dinner."

Patrolling the town almost felt like simply going for a walk as far as Montoya was concerned. Coyote Bluffs had grown over the course of Sheriff Weaver's career, but it was still a township, and you couldn't yet call it a city. Would that come later? Perhaps, but not in this lifetime. It had grown to the point where everybody didn't know everybody anymore, but those who had either been in town all their lives or who had added something vital to the town, like the first telegraph operator, everybody knew them.

They approached Johnny Moss, who had been operating the town bank for most of his adult life, which wasn't that long considering that he was only twenty-five years old. Montoya and Weaver came upon him as he was returning to the shop after taking lunch to his aging mother. "Afternoon Sheriff Weaver, Deputy Montoya."

"I'm leaving tomorrow, Johnny. At this point I'd say he's the sheriff." Weaver smiled as he gestured to Montoya. "If you got to call someone deputy, I guess that'd be me."

"Aw Hell. You've been sheriff since I was about this high." Johnny Moss held up his hand at about his thigh height. "Whether or not it's official, I think I'll call you sheriff till the day I kick. That being said, we're all real happy to have you here, Sheriff Montoya."

Montoya tipped his hat to Johnny. "I appreciate that Mr. Moss, and I hope to earn that kind of trust in you and others that I'll see to this town just like Sheriff Weaver here has been doing."

"How's your mother doing?" Weaver asked.

"She's doing alright." Johnny shrugged. "Doesn't get out as much as she used to since she's getting on in years. She's been helping my daughter set up her first little herb garden.

Weaver considered a moment. "I'll be sure to call on her one last time before I head on out of town. She won't be the only one. I don't know if or when I'll ever return to Coyote Bluffs, so I've got to make the rounds."

"Aw, don't say it like that sheriff, even if it's true."

Sheriff Weaver smiled and started to walk away. "You never can tell. But you know what they say. You can take a man out of Coyote Bluffs, but you can never take Coyote Bluffs out of a man."

Johnny laughed. "Nobody says that."

"Hell, I do." Weaver countered as he and Montoya continued on their way through the humble but harmonious town.

As they continued to walk through the town, Montoya couldn't help but notice how everyone in town from newcomers to old timers who'd been there even longer than Weaver seemed to regard them with comfort and trust in their hearts. It made him sad how in past posts both as a lawman and as a soldier, he felt like an occupying force keeping regular folk in line. Like many, he didn't see the difference between soldiering and policing at first. But after a few years, he saw that people didn't need a soldier looking after them. Hell, most of the time someone policing them wasn't the right thing either. What he wanted to be was something between a peacekeeper and a caretaker. That's the type of lawman that Weaver had been able to become, and judging by the scars the man carried, it wasn't always easy. But Montoya had casually asked around about Weaver's years as sheriff and whether it was an old timer talking or someone who'd only been around a year or two, nobody ever mentioned a time when Weaver let anger get in the way of justice, or let the law get in the way of knowing right from wrong. Montoya knew that in a larger town with more people and more police being that kind of a lawman didn't come easy, and he wondered if it would ever feel damn near impossible. He'd often thought about being sheriff of a bigger place, but in that moment, Coyote Bluffs was just fine with him since he could be the type of lawman he wanted to be.

They stopped by the church to see Father Gabriel, who Montoya noticed Sheriff Weaver sometimes accidentally called "Father Porter." Montoya didn't take it as a lack of knowing or the old sheriff's memory going. It seemed like when he said the title, "Father," the name Porter just seemed to follow, as it must have for years. Montoya didn't need to be told that Father Gabriel was relatively new to Coyote Bluffs. His excited but not yet comfortable demeanor said it all. Either way, the priest seemed like a kind enough man. In Montoya's experience, clergy either made him feel very peaceful and at ease, or they scared the hell out of him. Montoya liked Father Gabriel well enough, and imagined that in years to come, folks around town would see the two of them as part of the same generation of newcomers to Coyote Bluffs, even though their arrivals may have been separated by a few years, but once they were well behind you, a few years wasn't a whole lot.

Over the rest of the afternoon, Weaver and Montoya called on a few more people around town, but mostly they just walked around, seeing what there was to see and letting themselves be seen. It was less of a patrol and more of a reminder, reassuring the town that they were there. The sun had begun to sink into the mountainous horizon by the time the two returned to Weaver's small, but comfortable home.

Weaver threw a couple thick steaks onto a cast iron skillet along with a few chopped up onions and a poblano pepper, which he handled carefully. "How do you take your steak, Montoya?"

"Rare enough that I may have to chase it down before I can eat it." Manuel smiled.

"Good answer." Weaver flipped the steaks over. "In my experience, you never trust a man who wants his steak cooked like you dipped it in the lake of fire." After tending to the meal for a few short minutes, Weaver divided the contents of the cast-iron pan across two plates. He sat down and placed one of the plates in front of Manuel. "Alright. Where was I?"

Manuel looked across the humble but well appointed home. "I apologize if I'm overstepping by asking, but when did your wife pass?"

Sheriff Weaver feigned shock, but saw exactly what had led Manuel to assume he was a widower. "Mrs. Weaver is up in Colorado with my son and his wife. I'll be joining them once we're finished here and I officially pass the reins over to you."

"Were you married back then?" Montoya, a bachelor, asked.

"No. I decided a long time ago that I ought to establish myself in life before asking a woman to be such a big part of it, and at the time, I was a younger man. I'd barely been sheriff of Coyote Bluffs for a year when this all started.

He sat down and cut a fatty end piece of the steak and gnawed on it before swallowing it in a big gulp. "So like I was saying, Theodore Watkins struck rich and the town grew, but nobody knew why. I still walked the widow, Isabelle Mills and her twins, Johnny and Elizabeth to the school house each morning. The preacher, Remy Porter, still gave his sermons Sunday and spent the rest of the week seeing to the sickly and the poor. I still mostly handled drunks and the occasional dispute over one of the smaller gold finds, but even that was starting to go by the wayside. With Watkins buying up all the smaller finds, there wasn't much to dispute."

"So far that doesn't sound too bad," Manuel said through the crunch of the peppers and onions.

"Things didn't really go south until Watkins tried to do the right thing on his own. He shut down his gold mine and used the money he'd made to pay former miners to guard the entrance with rifles at the ready."

"That sounds like the recipe for trouble," Montoya added. "Armed men, and a whole lot of money just sitting there."

"There were some troubles, of course. Clayton Rhodes got a few men together and there was a standoff between them and the guards to try to get in. I had to get between the groups and work it out to keep them from blowing each other to kingdom come. After that, Watkins went into the mine himself and used dynamite to bury it all back in the stomach of the earth where it should have stayed, and believe it or not, the mine stayed shut down for weeks. Lots of folks left town, save for them who were here before it was a rich place and a few others. Some of the folks that stayed wouldn't have surprised you. Holden Quinn stayed. He owns the hardware shop in town now, but back then he came out here to strike it rich and the mine shut down right when his wife, Angela, and daughter Anne came to live with him. He wasn't about to move his family right after getting set up in a new home. There were some surprises too, like Miles Hopkins. He came to the town to get rich like lots of other folks, but for whatever reason he decided to stay. Maybe when you find the place that's meant to be your home, you just feel it."

"Is that how it was for you?" Manuel asked, looking at the warm glow of the sheriff's humble home and imagining the love that emanated from it when he was there with his family all those years.

"It'd be pretty to say so, but that wasn't the case for me," Dallas Weaver replied, almost disappointed in his own answer. "You'd think this place meant everything to me, given that I'd been sheriff here for longer than some folks even lived. No. For me, it's about the people. I walked Johnny and Elizabeth Mills to school when they were little and now I watch them walk their own kids to the school house. It's those kind of things that make a place feel like home. Without my wife, my boy, and the other folks who came up in Coyote Bluffs, this is just a patch of land like any other."

Montoya digested both the steak and Weaver's words. The town hadn't become his home yet, but he knew it would be, and thanks to the old sheriff, he knew how it would come to feel that way. Getting to know the people who made up Coyote Bluffs, making them family. That's what would make being sheriff feel more like a calling and less like a job.

"It was then, that things took a turn," Weaver explained, his demeanor becoming more grave. "Instead of Watkins coming to the wolf each night, it would come to him. Appear by his bedside. Telling him that burying what he'd unearthed was a mistake and one that all of Coyote Bluffs would pay for dearly."

"That's when the real trouble started." Montoya shuddered.

Sheriff Weaver nodded. "The first of the plagues to come upon Coyote Bluffs came in the form of a thunderstorm that lasted two weeks. The ground here isn't made to soak up that much water, so for most of that time, the good people of Coyote Bluffs were holed up in their houses, avoiding the streets which had become rivers of disease and horse shit. Lots of folks thought that would be the worst of it, but they would've been wrong. The storm was just there to wear us down. To make it that much harder to handle what would come next."

"What came next?" Manuel Montoya asked. "You make it sound like something out of the bible."

"If you were to describe it that way, you wouldn't be wrong," Weaver sighed. "The rain stopped and folks cleaned up the town, but then a sickness spread through the town."

"Brought on by the filth of the flood?" Montoya asked.

"Brought on by him," Weaver corrected. "We thought the same way you did at first. But then we had to ask ourselves why it was only the children that caught it. Sure. The schoolhouse is a place where disease can spread, but so is a saloon and none of the drunks were falling ill. The town doctor didn't know what to make of it. None of us did, until Watkins finally came to me and told me what had happened to him out in the forest," Weaver sighed with regret. "Of course, I didn't believe him at first. Who would? My thought was that maybe there was some truth to what he said, but no talking wolves or biblical plagues. Maybe there was a man out there in the forest who stood to gain by having Watkins take over the gold find. Maybe he was the one who killed Boyd and I missed some vital clue after I talked with Moss and had a good enough explanation. Maybe that man was intimidating Watkins into keeping quiet. So I humored him. I went out to the forest where he said the wolf would be."

Montoya leaned in more closely. "And?"

"At first, I went out there with a stealthy approach, hoping I'd see them before they saw me, but after a few nights freezing my ass off in the creek with nothing to show for it, I decided to be more bold," Weaver smirked, amused with his younger self. "The last night I walked right into the open where Watkins said he'd seen the wolf, hand on my pistol like it was a showdown, which I suppose it was."

"And the wolf?" Montoya nearly fell out of his chair from leaning forward, as if being closer to Weaver would get him to tell the next part faster. "Did you see it?"

"Come walking up out of the shadows, like he owned the place." Sheriff Weaver patted his palm against the pistol still holstered on his hip, an old Colt revolver that was likely older than Montoya, and just as reliable. "I stood there, hand on my gun and waited for it to get closer. It never bared its teeth or growled. It just walked forward like a man looking to have a conversation."

"'You are real.' That was all I could muster. The thing approached me and I thought that it was going to sniff at me like any normal wolf would, but it never did. It circled me like a predator closing in on its prey. That was when I noticed that the matted fur kept moving, almost like the wind was blowing, violent and sporadic, but it wasn't. The night was as still as this one. It was like its skin never stopped crawling like flames licking at a log. Finally, it stopped when it had made its way behind me and I thought that it would pounce at any moment."

"It didn't," Manuel stated, sure that if it had, he wouldn't be talking to Weaver at this moment.

Weaver took in air and leaned back in his chair. "No. It waited there until I turned around to face it. It didn't talk, not the way you'd think. It was like having a thought in your head that wasn't your own, and the words hit like a punch in the gut. It asked what I wanted. I asked its name."

"What did it say?" Montoya asked, surprised that he'd come to believe a story so outlandish so quickly.

"It told me that man couldn't utter the beast's true name, and when I said I wanted to hear it, not say it, it came up with a sound. Something between a growl and a crackling fire. It was right. Its name was a sound that mankind wasn't meant to hear. The second I heard it, I staggered backward with a headache to match a ten-tequila hangover and my nose started to bleed."

"Jesus." Montoya crossed himself.

"Jesus ain't got nothing to do with that thing in the desert." Weaver swallowed hard. "It asked again what I wanted and I told him that I wanted him and his influence out of Coyote Bluffs forever. It charged at me, but I figured it would eventually, so I had put enough distance between me and him that I could draw and fire my pistol twice before it could reach me." Weaver hesitated. "I hope by now you realize that I ain't one of those pistoleros that boasts that they could hit a playing card nailed to a tree at fifty yards. I ain't that and I never was, so when I tell you that there was no way I could've missed I say it because it was a big damned target and I wasn't more than fifteen yards from it, less on the second shot."

"What did it do to you?"

"It leaped up and pinned me down. At first, it did what wolves usually do. It went for my throat. Lucky for me, I was able to raise up my arm in time, so it just took a good chunk out of my forearm instead of out of my neck." Weaver rolled up his shirt sleeve to reveal a deep and jagged scar, a continent on a roadmap of pain. "That wasn't the worst of its onslaught though. As it leaped off of me and repositioned itself to attack again from another angle, I looked down and I was covered in a dozen scorpions! I don't know how, but there was no natural way those things could have climbed up on me in the middle of a wolf attack. I scrambled to my feet and swatted at them with my good hand, and with every one I crushed, it burst into liquid fire almost like a burning jam on my chest. By the time I tore off my vest and let it burn at my feet, the wolf was in a wide set stance ready for another go."

"If your first two shots didn't do anything, how did you beat it?" Manuel felt the awe that he'd been filled with as a child in church back in Mexico when he'd heard stories of warrior angels defending Heaven.

"I didn't," Weaver sighed. "It came at me again, and even though I was able to dodge out of the way and take a shot at its flank from less than a yard away, it didn't even flinch. That's when I knew for sure that I wasn't ready to protect the town from whatever this thing was, so I ran. I know some folks might not see that as exactly heroic, but I wouldn't have been able to do a damn thing for the town if I was dead. So I ran, and I'm sure it let me get away just to spread the fear."

"What happened when you got back to town?" Montoya leaned forward in his chair eagerly.

Sheriff Weaver stood up and put on his coat. "Speaking of getting back to town, let's do another patrol. I'll wrap up the story once we've given the township a good once over."

This time Weaver followed Montoya on their rounds of the township. This would be their last time doing so together, and it was important to Weaver to hand over the reins as much as he could before leaving town. By this point, most people had finished their work for the day, except the barkeep at the local saloon and the innkeeper, who could almost always be found at the front desk of the town's one and only hotel, a humble but charming inn. Still, the two men made sure to greet, or at least tip their hats to anyone still out on the thoroughfare they crossed paths with. The wonder and worry over how Weaver survived his encounter with the wolf itched at the back of Montoya's mind, but he knew better than to ask about it out in the open. It wasn't ever specifically said, but from the moment Weaver had begun telling the tale, Montoya got the impression that it wasn't the sort of thing he went around telling everyone. Montoya figured that when he was a few years into being sheriff, he might be able to bring it up with some of the old timers, the ones who'd been there at the time, but he knew he hadn't earned that yet.

"Hang back a minute," Weaver said as they approached a wooden house on a hill. "That's the widow Moss's house. I'm going to go up and make sure she won't mind someone besides me calling on her. If she's doing alright, I'll call you on up. If not, just head on back to the house and I'll see you later."

Montoya nodded and waited for Weaver to go up to the house and return. He tried to look like he was busy doing something, anything besides just standing around waiting for the widow Moss's permission to come up and call on her. It was in moments such as these that Montoya envied men who'd taken up smoking pipes. They always seemed to have something to do with their hands if they were stuck standing around outdoors for a while. Montoya, on the other hand, hooked his thumbs in the pockets of his pants and looked around and didn't see a whole hell of a lot.

Just as Montoya considered possibly heading on back to the house, Weaver stepped outside onto Mrs. Moss's porch. "Come on up, Montoya."

He followed Weaver in to find a house bigger than a woman would need to live alone, but then again, Mrs. Moss hadn't lived there alone. She'd been there with her husband and the twins, and when the twins were grown, she kept a room ready for her granddaughter to stay whenever she needed to. It was a well taken care of house, clean and orderly. The house was built solid and still looked sturdy, despite the creaks and cracks of age beginning to show, which is just about how Montoya would have described Mrs. Moss. If he had to guess, he'd put her at about eighty-years old, but with a wellspring of strength that never seemed to deplete, just waiting for when she needed it most.

Montoya removed his hat as he entered the doorway. "Evening, ma'am."

"Evening. My son says he crossed paths with you two earlier."

Sheriff Weaver sat down at her table as if he'd done so a thousand times. "That we did, Mrs. Moss. He tells us you're helping his daughter with her herb garden."

"I am. Can't learn it from either of her parents. Those two couldn't keep a plant alive if their lives depended on it."

"Thankfully, it don't." Weaver chuckled.

Her chuckle turned into a cough that made Montoya wonder if it were just a dry cough, or a prelude to something worse. "They'll be alright, but their pork roast will suffer unless the little one learns how to grow rosemary, and thyme before I kick."

They both laughed. Montoya laughed along, mostly because it simply felt like the thing to do. Weaver leaned in a little bit closer. "I am grateful that you showed my wife how to make a rub for that pork with rosemary and thyme. Here's hoping it grows the same up Colorado way."

"I don't want to sound selfish, but I hate to see you go, Sheriff."

"I'm halfway sorry to leave. Don't you worry though. You'll have Sheriff Montoya here." Weaver patted Montoya on the arm approvingly.

She leaned toward Weaver. "Does he know about the..." Mrs. Moss trailed off.

"I'm telling him." Weaver cut her off before she had to speak out loud something she'd rather not. "You needn't worry. Montoya will keep you and your kin safe from any danger that rears its head in Coyote Bluffs."

Montoya did his best to conceal his concern that there might be some kind of threat like the one Weaver had been telling him about. Up until that moment, Montoya had assumed that whatever Weaver told him about was something that had already begun and ended over twenty years earlier. Both of his elders saw right through the facade. "It's alright," Weaver said to both of them. "You and yours will be there to back Sheriff Montoya just like he'll be there to back you. Same as it ever was."

"Same as it ever was," Mrs. Moss replied as she sunk back into her chair.

"We've got to get back to the house now," Weaver said. "I need to finish packing up my things, and Montoya needs to finish hearing about that other thing. Goodbye, Mrs. Moss."

"Goodnight, Dallas."

Upon returning to his front porch, Sheriff Weaver sat in the familiar rocking chair on his front porch and gestured for Manuel to sit in the chair next to him where everyone from his wife, to deputies, or just folks around town who needed to talk had taken a seat. "I got on my horse and tried to get the hell out of there, but a rattlesnake shot out from under a rock and bit her on the ankle. I didn't know at the time, but I cracked three ribs when I fell. I tried to help her up, but the wolf caught up quick and tore out the horse's throat in an instant. When I turned to say something, two golden snakes slithered out from inside the wound and grew into more wolves and when I saw that, I turned tail and ran the miles back to town without looking back once."

Montoya looked at Weaver the way he looked at old veterans of battles he knew to be among the most horrific that war had to offer. He respected the service that Weaver had done for Coyote Bluffs already, but now his respect extended to what the man was willing to endure and keep going.

"When I got back into town, I could hardly breathe, let alone speak. I must have passed out, because the next thing I knew, it was dawn and I was at the Widow Mills' house and her twins were looking me over curiously. When little Elizabeth called out that I'd opened my eyes, the town doctor came quickly and told me not to sit up too fast. I'd lost a lot of blood, but he'd managed to patch me up in time to save my arm and my life. I scanned my surroundings and when I saw the sun had come up, I breathed a sigh of relief. Nobody had ever seen the wolf in the daylight hours. I didn't tell the doctor what I'd seen right away. I figured that if I told him all that, he'd start checking me for head injuries instead of helping me figure out what we could possibly do to stop it. Instead I told him to get Watkins, and the mayor, and to meet me over at the church where Father Porter would be. Before I could even get up, Mrs. Moss insisted that she and her little ones come along. Now I've never been one to think that there's anything a man can handle that a woman can't, but I knew that the children had no place hearing what I was planning on saying, but she wasn't interested in my opinion on that matter. She insisted that she and her children were part of this since they were the ones who found me face down on the edge of town and whatever happened to Coyote Bluffs was as much their business as anyone else's."

"Strong woman," Manuel smirked. "Reminds me of my mother."

Dallas Weaver smiled at the thought of a strong woman raising the man he sat next to. "We headed to the church where Father Porter was already waiting for us. Mrs. Moss sent her son to run ahead and tell him we were coming and that there was trouble. He brought us inside, lit a few candles and said a prayer before having us sit in some of the pews where he asked what had happened."

"Did he believe you?" Montoya asked.

"He came around more quickly than I did. I suppose a preacher is bound to have more faith than a lawman. He said the devil was at work in our little town. I told him that I hoped he was wrong, that the wolf represented some lesser form of evil. Something I could handle. He just nodded. By the time the doctor caught up to us with the mayor and Watkins, a few others had come just to see what the commotion was all about. I told them what had happened. Watkins backed me, and for those that didn't believe, they had to take the chunk bit out of my arm, the burn marks on my torso, and the horse blood spattered on my boots as evidence enough. I explained to them that all the things that had been happening in Coyote Bluffs lately had been plagues visited upon us by whatever evil had taken the form of a wolf on the edge of town. We came up with a plan."

"What was it?" Manuel asked, focused as if he were taking notes for his own tenure as sheriff.

Sheriff Weaver leaned back and exhaled sharply. "You got to understand, we were desperate. We knew the wolf wasn't gonna stop until we were doing his bidding or until we were dead. That, and we knew a .44 caliber revolver did less than nothing to it. We all racked our brains trying to think of anything we knew that had even a chance of affecting it. He wasn't sure if it was sacrilege, but he blessed my bullets. He let me fill my canteen with holy water. Mrs. Moss said she knew a woman back east who'd told her that some creatures not of this world could be hurt by iron. I don't have to tell you my bullets weren't made of iron, so she gave me the iron fire poker from her house. Miles Hopkins, a prospector who'd been up north in Indian country gave me some herbs that he'd been told would ward off evil. I don't know what they were, but I stuck a handful of them in my jacket pocket. We didn't know if they'd do anything, but I knew I had to try something, for the sake of the town."

"Sounds like you were marching off to a battle you weren't expecting to return from."

Weaver glanced down at his boots and then up again. "Since we're sitting here, you know that ain't how it turned out, but at the time, that's exactly what I was thinking. I made my peace with the folks around town. I told the drunks I'd hauled in that they weren't bad guys, and I told Mrs. Moss that I hope she raises up those twins to be good people. Watkins stood at the edge of town, waiting for me like."

Sheriff Weaver stood up and shook out his left leg, a habit that Montoya had noted and assumed that maybe it got a bit stiff when a storm was coming due to an injury he'd sustained years back. "Watkins said he was going to go with me. He told me that he started this and it was his responsibility to try to put a stop to it. I told him that it wasn't his fault. The force that guided him to that gold claim was something that had been out there in the desert longer than people had, maybe longer than good and evil. Hell, maybe that force and how we seen it is what made good and evil." His voice trailed off. "I don't mean to say that good and evil was come up with in Texas. I believe for a certainty that forces like the one that took the form of a wolf in our town existed in many corners of our world. Maybe it's the responsibility of good people to keep it at bay...Anyways, that's what I was going to try to do. It felt a bit like trying to stop the tide from coming in. You ever been to the ocean, Montoya?"

"Yeah." He smiled. "When my parents and me came up from Mexico when I was a boy, we were on the west coast. We came up through California before settling in Texas. On the trek north, the ocean was always to my left."

Weaver shrugged. "I never seen it. Maybe I'll head out that way with the missus one day. If the devil is in the desert, maybe God is in the ocean."

"I don't believe that," Manuel stated strongly.

"What do you believe?"

"I think God is everywhere and so is the devil, and it's up to us to find good, to be good, and to keep evil at bay."

"Yeah." Weaver smiled. "I like that. Still might take Mrs. Weaver to the ocean though. Neither of us ever seen it and I'd say it's about time."

"So what happened out there in the desert?" Manuel's patience had begun to fray.

"Right. I got Lydia Hewitt to loan me her husband's horse and I rode out there on my own with whatever blessings, and weapons I could cobble together. When I got to the spot where the forest and the desert met, I got down from the horse and let it go. I saw what happened to the last one, and I knew that the only way a horse could help me would be to escape, and I had no thought of that. I was either going to overcome what was waiting for me, or...well, I wouldn't be walking back to town. The sun dipped below the horizon, and soon enough, the wolf come up over the hill."

Sheriff Weaver stood and looked off into the distance from his porch. "So I stood there, hand on my pistol, but I didn't draw it. It walked up and I don't know how it could with a wolf's mouth, but it smirked at me." He sat back down in his rocking chair, aware of how worn out he felt. "Like it did before, it spoke to me without speaking. The words just came into my mind, into my soul, and each word felt like a punch in the gut. It told me that I wasn't going to stop it. That I was going to do what it wanted me to. It told me to go open up that mine, go back into town and shoot Watkins in the knee. He put the image in my mind of me doing it and it felt so good, but I knew it wasn't coming from me, wasn't coming from anywhere good. I pushed it out of my mind and focused on where I was. I knew that if I gave the wolf any more time in my mind than I'd already had then I'd do something, become something that you wouldn't recognize. So I did something. Something that to this day I can't decide whether it was very smart or very stupid. I drew my pistol and fired. One of the bullets that Father Porter had blessed hit it right between the eyes."

"Did it work?" Montoya leaned in so far he was almost off the edge of his chair.

"Sort of," Weaver replied. "It flinched. You know and I know that probably the most surefire way to kill anything is to put a .44 caliber bullet right into its head, but damn. I've had sneezes that caused me more pain than the wolf showed. Still...it did react. It did something. The wolf charged at me with the intention of ending the confrontation before it could begin. Before, it was just toying with me, like a cat pawing at a wounded mouse before finally going in for the kill when it stopped fighting. The wolf wasn't having fun with me. It saw me as a threat that it meant to destroy with all of the power and ferocity that it could muster."

Weaver held up his horrifically scarred forearm. "It lunged for my throat and I held up this arm again, which it intended to tear off. The only reason it didn't was because I soaked my bandage in the holy water I'd put in my canteen. It didn't hurt it, but it seemed like it didn't like the taste. That brief moment of hesitation gave me enough time to pull the hammer back on my pistol and fire another shot, this time into its gut. Just like before, it only seemed to piss it off, but that was all I could do. I rolled onto my side to get it off of me, and unloaded the remaining four shots into its flank. The black flames of its form started to sink into the dry earth, and for a second there I thought that maybe I'd killed it, but when I turned around, it was already waiting for me in the shadows of the forest. It charged again, and this time I was out of ammo."

"The iron fire poker!" Montoya exclaimed. "You finished him off with that!"

"You're half right," Weaver smirked. "I held up the fire poker in front of me. It was all I had left to protect myself with. When it lunged at me, I held each end of the poker and shoved the middle of it right into its maw."

"Did it work?"

"Worked as well as hitting anything with an iron rod would. I don't know if it was because the stories Mrs. Moss had heard were right, or because that's just what happens when you hit something with a five-pound iron rod. Either way, it was keeping the wolf from tearing me to shreds. It tore at me and I held it at bay with the iron, but soon enough it overpowered me. I lost my grip with my left hand when it pawed at my wounded arm, and it tore the poker out of my hands and got off me before taking a wide stance between me and the iron rod. The only hope I saw was that maybe by some miracle I could keep it off me until I could reload my pistol. I tried to run into the trees where maybe I could find enough cover to find time to reload."

Weaver rubbed his worn hands on his right leg, the one that looked like it'd been aching before. "I didn't make it five paces before fire shot straight out of the ground and up my right leg to the knee. Fast as I was going, I fell down pretty hard and it took me a minute to get my coat off to try to use it to put out the flames. I patted at the flames frantically, but another swarm of scorpions came pouring out of every fold of fabric. They crawled up my arm, stinging me and sending the burn of that fire up the length of my right arm. The wolf had begun toying with me again. It had disarmed me, and I was no longer a threat to it. I looked into its empty eyes and knew that it wanted to show me every horror it could before it finished me off."

"How'd you beat it?"

"I didn't. It had me dead to rights, and just when it was about to finish me off, a crack of gunfire split the air, and it flew back in a hail of bullets that Father Porter had given the same treatment as mine." Weaver waved his hand across the landscape that made up Coyote Bluffs township. "Everyone from Watkins himself, to Mrs. Moss and even Father Porter had taken up arms against the evil that threatened our home. Even the Moss twins stood shoulder to shoulder with the prospectors, farmers, and other folk that have come to call Coyote Bluffs home. I half expected the mayor or Father Porter to step up and say something, but it wasn't them. Mrs. Moss stepped up and shouted for the wolf to go back where it had come from and never to bring harm to the people of our town again. 'The sheriff has backed us and we'll back him,' she said. 'If you want Coyote Bluffs, then you're gonna have to take on every last one of us and you may kill us, but then you won't have dominion over nothing but a patch of dirt with nobody to call it home!' I swear I never heard someone speak with such force. The way the wolf's words hit like a blow...her words must have done the same to him, because it turned tail and disappeared into the darkness of the desert, and that's where it's been since."

Montoya thought for a long time about what Weaver told him. Of course, it was unbelievable at first, but at that moment, Manuel simply leaned back in the old rocking chair wearing a face as if he'd just eaten something that he couldn't decide whether or not he liked it.

"What's the matter?" Weaver asked.

"You said it was the one time you were the one who saved the town. But it wasn't you." As Manuel said the words, he didn't know what to make of them.

"It's never just one man that saves nothing," Weaver chuckled. "Even if you do it by yourself, you're carrying the strength of them you fight for. Truth be told I don't think that you, me, or anyone could have taken it on by themselves. It wouldn't have mattered if I'd've brought a damned cannon with me to that fight. If it weren't for the folks that made up Coyote Bluffs standing together, we wouldn't have been able to banish the beast back to the wilds from which it came."

Montoya digested Weaver's final lesson. "If it takes everyone together to stand against the darkness, then what's my role in this? What am I supposed to take from that about being a good sheriff?"

"Oh I don't know." Weaver stood up from his chair and walked down the creaky wooden steps onto the ground. "Maybe that it's more important to bring folks together, and to know who you're fighting for."

Insecurity gripped Montoya's normally insurmountable confidence. "But I don't know these people like you do."

Weaver smiled. "You will. Until then, they'll be the ones that have your back."

Montoya took in the lesson. "I guess you're right. You still leaving tomorrow morning?"

"Sure am." Weaver started walking to where his horse was stabled. "Heading out of here at first light, but come with me. There's something we got to do first."

The two men got on their horses and Montoya followed Weaver west, out of the township and into the desert. The town had expanded in the days since Weaver was a young sheriff and it wasn't ten minutes before Weaver stopped at a patch of land where the desert and the forest met. The old sheriff got down from his horse and led it forward a few paces where he gazed into the vast and unknowable darkness before him. He looked back at Montoya and nodded for him to get down from his horse and do the same. Manuel climbed down and stood by the old sheriff proudly.

When they stood shoulder to shoulder, Dallas Weaver turned and stared down the darkness. "I know you're still out here, you son of a bitch. I been waiting for you all these years, and don't you think that this town ain't protected just because I'm leaving. The town's got Montoya, the Moss twins, and every other good person who makes it up. You stay out here, hiding in the desert. Stay out here where you belong, and if you come sniffing around our home, you'll find us all waiting for you. Same as it ever was."

"Same as it ever was," Montoya repeated with the reverence of prayer.

"Tell him, kid."

Sheriff Montoya stood taller than he ever had before and he bellowed into the darkness. "My name is Sheriff Manuel Montoya. That name means mountain and that's exactly how I'll stand by the people of this town. Firm and unmovable, like a mountain, and when I earn it, they'll do the same for me and there won't be nothing a beast like you can do to destroy that."

They stood and stared out into the desert, both palming their holstered revolvers, ready for whatever may come. The darkness remained in the dark and Weaver climbed back on his horse and led Montoya back to the town he'd go on to be sheriff of the rest of his days.

The sun crept from behind the cover of the horizon and Montoya finished helping the old sheriff load what remained of his worldly possessions onto a humble wagon. He bid his mentor farewell and watched him ride north to his family and to a well earned rest.

Weaver rode away from Coyote Bluffs knowing that he'd never return, but also knowing that he'd never need to, because when you become a part of a place, it becomes a part of you. He'd live the rest of his days on this earth with the strength lent to him by the people he protected, and with an eye on the darkening horizon for what he knew lay in wait.

Before the Mountain Was Born

Two men sat on horseback, dirty from three days riding ahead of the camp they'd come from and had been set up to work on the railroad. Johnny Duffy, an Irishman who'd proven himself the past few years, worked the railways and had become something of a scout. Dan Brown who'd just been hired to help Johnny scout ahead to make sure there weren't any obstacles that would slow down the laying of railroad tracks before the rest of the company caught up and set up camp. A series of small mountains that some might call hills out West stood before them and to their left there lay a forest as old as the land itself and beyond that a cliff's edge leading to a ravine where a creek ran through. They examined the land for a long time, considering the best way that the inevitable railroad could traverse the untamed land as efficiently as possible.

"That mountain is old as this land, but that don't mean we can't get through it," Johnny Duffy said as he and Dan Brown stared up at the mountain. "The bosses would rather we blast on through than direct the tracks out of the way to find a pass on our own. Besides, you saw that cliff a few hundred feet south of here. Anything could go wrong with that. If someone thinks to dam up that little creek, the tracks would end up too close to the water. If the tracks go through here, the most they'll have to deal with is a mighty fine view of a lake. Trust me. Blasting our way through is the right move."

"You sure about that?" Dan asked. He had a tendency to involve the bosses far more often than Burns would have liked, but if there was one thing Dan knew, it was the sheer extent of how much he didn't know. "Might be that going round is cheaper and easier."

"I very much doubt that Daniel Brown," Duffy jabbed back, running his fingers through his curly red hair. He only used Dan's full name when he felt fully confident in what he was about to say. "I been with the railroad company a lot longer than you and I've seen us blast through more than my fair share of mountain passes just like this one. They always want to blast through instead of rerouting the whole track. Maybe it's because they don't want to have to lay a longer track than what they'd planned, or maybe it's because they don't want nobody, not even God to get in the way. All I can tell you is that if you take the time to ask the bosses, they're going to tell you just what I'm telling you, and they'll be right pissed off for you having wasted their time asking."

It didn't take much more than that for Johnny to convince Dan to get the rest of the team up there ready to blast their way through the mountain. They'd seen the same scene played out plenty of times and were fully prepared for the noise and the dust and the danger. What they weren't prepared for was the single oval of a dark stone standing solitary where the rest of the mountain had been blasted away.

"What in the Hell?" Dan's jaw hung open wide despite the dust blowing in his direction.

Johnny wiped the sweat from his brow and approached the stone that stood at least seven feet tall, staring at it as if unsure that what he saw was real. "This whole chunk of mountain blasted to dust, and this thing's sitting here untouched, looking like the earth itself laid an egg."

"Johnny, if we're standing around where the earth laid an egg, wouldn't that put us at the ass-end of the world?"

"You saying we ain't?" Johnny waved for Dan to join him near the rock. "Grab one of them pickaxes and come on over here."

The two men hit it with pickaxes, tried to dig it out with shovels, and even tried blasting the shiny black stone again. None of their efforts left so much as a scratch on it. The only markings it had were the ones that had been there since they first saw it. It didn't look like any sort of writing either of the men had ever seen, and after some convincing, Dan finally got Johnny to agree that they needed to tell the bosses about it.

The company sent out a man named Bertram Corbitt, a geologist to examine the stone. Normally Corbitt had been called upon to a particular area to see if there were valuable minerals in the ground. Hearing about a stone that neither pickaxe nor dynamite could destroy excited him. If he could be the one to attach his name to the discovery of such a material, he could really make a name for himself in the scientific community. It took less than a week for him to reach them.

"Are you the gentlemen who found the mineral?" Bertram wore a three-piece suit with a gold chain leading to a pocket watch in his vest pocket. He wore a bowler hat that did more to cover his balding scalp than to keep the sun off him and a well-maintained mustache sat atop his pursed lips. "I'm Mr. Corbitt, the geologist sent to examine your find."

Johnny regarded the man for a moment before answering. "I'm Johnny Duffy and this here's Dan Brown. And yeah. We were blasting a path through the mountain and this one rock just wouldn't budge. Strange looking thing too. I ain't never seen anything like it. It's black and glassy, and nothing we did to it made a single scratch on it."

"That's right, sir," Dan added. "The markings were on it when we found it."

The mention of markings piqued Bertram's interest. If none of their tools or even explosives could put a mark on this substance, then what could have made markings on it? "Would you gentlemen be so kind as to take me to the find now?"

Bertram Corbitt examined the stone and at first he thought it might have been obsidian, but that didn't seem right because it couldn't have stood up to the railroad workers trying to remove it. He thought the markings were strange and didn't even begin to think about what they meant, but rather how they were put there. It didn't look scratched into the surface of the stone, and the markings were too specific to have been eroded naturally over time. The indentations that made the markings looked almost like they had been melted into the stone, which seemed impossible. While he was no expert on written languages, Bertram couldn't help but look at the markings, convinced that the markings were repetitive and intentional enough that they hadn't gotten there by accident. He imagined some early society somehow putting these marks into the stone...somehow, but from his cursory analysis, the stone had been beneath the mountain far too long for that to be possible. All of this seemed highly unlikely to Mr. Corbitt, but there it was staring back at him.

"What do you think?" Johnny slapped the round stone and leaned up against it.

Corbitt stared up at the top of the stone, not bothering to make eye contact with Johnny. "I'd like to take a sample back, but it seems like taking a sample will be a difficult task."

"Maybe you'll have to take the whole damn thing, just pluck it up out of the earth," Dan offered. "You think there's a chance it goes down further than what we see? Like the roots of a tree or something?"

Bertram didn't want to spend too much time taking Dan's idea seriously, but frankly, for all he knew Dan could have been right. "It's a consideration I'll have to make."

"What about them marks on it? Are they there naturally or did someone put them there?" Johnny asked.

Corbitt stood back and unsuccessfully tried to keep his tone from sounding condescending. "Sir, I can assure you that no man 'put them there' as you put it. This feature has been buried beneath the mountain since before man stood upright."

Johnny didn't know quite what Corbitt meant, but he understood his tone completely. "What's that supposed to mean?"

Bertram managed his tone, reminding himself that these were laypeople and they hadn't had the benefit of the education he'd been blessed to receive. "It means that the last time this rock saw the light of day, there weren't any people to have made the markings."

"You mean it ain't native?" Dan asked.

"Ain't you heard the man? He said there weren't no people here last time this thing was out in the open." Johnny scolded. "If that's true, then who was there when these markings were made?"

"Only God, the creatures that walked the earth when it was young, and…" his voice trailed off.

"And what?"

Bertram Corbitt shuddered and tried not to think about some primordial society of inhuman beings forgotten by history, and perhaps rightly so. "I don't know, and I'm not sure I want to find out."

There followed a long pause and an understanding between Johnny and Bertram that the conversation had ended, but Dan wasn't there yet.

"Just the same, it might not have been made by the local tribes, but maybe they seen something like it before. They been here longer than us. If it walks, crawls, or slithers on this land, they seen it," Dan insisted.

Corbitt sighed copiously. "I know a man from one of the local tribes back in Denver. His name is...well, nobody can pronounce his name quite right, but he told us it means moon, so we've taken to calling him, Moon. He seems to accept it. I suppose that when I have the stone photographed and examined by various experts, I could show it to him. Perhaps he, or his ancestors have seen something like this before. Just the same, I believe showing it around at the university could glean results as well."

Johnny and Dan gave one another a concerned glance. Johnny broke the silence. "Do you know how to get rid of it? That what the railroad company wants. We're just here to scout ahead and make sure the path is cleared. The rest of the company is set to arrive any day now and they need to be able to get to work."

Bertram grew tired of listening to Johnny and Dan speak. They'd stumbled upon a mineral that in all his years of education he hadn't even read about, much less seen, and all they cared about was getting it out of the way to make room for a train. "Gentlemen, I hate to disappoint your employers, but it will take significantly less time and fewer resources to simply go around it. I do, however, suggest that you go around it on the northern side. If the vibrations of passing trains shake some of the earth free, you want a large stone like that to fall away from the tracks, not onto them."

"So you mean we ain't gonna move it." Dan frowned.

Corbitt looked at Dan as if he were a petulant child. "Perhaps it isn't meant to be moved. Perhaps something wants it there, something older than the mountain." Corbitt left with his photographs and notes.

The next morning neither Johnny nor Dan ever saw him again. They did, however, lean on his testimony heavily when the rest of the company arrived and griped at the thought of circumnavigating the egg-shaped stone blocking their intended path.

Once the laborers arrived and started laying tracks, something always seemed to be going wrong. At first, things went unnoticed by everyone except Johnny and Dan. Tools broke more often than they should, the weather always seeming to be against them. It wasn't uncommon for some laborers to leave the railroad camp in search of better opportunities, or simply because they knew that if they stayed, they'd end up working themselves to death on train tracks they'd never see finished, but normally men who did that always did so right after a payday, and never during bad weather. These rules no longer seemed to apply. Johnny couldn't find any rhyme or reason to why people were leaving the camp so randomly, until one night when he stayed up late to write a letter to his family back East by lantern light. He saw one of the workers from China standing in front of the stone, the symbols on it reflecting the moonlight giving it an eerie glow. The man was just staring up at it, not with reverence, or awe, but with eyes that were seeing something else. It struck Johnny as so strange that he stopped writing his letter and just watched the man.

He should have been asleep. The railroad company had worked this man to the bone for weeks. Instead he stood there in the dark, feeling neither the cold of the night nor the ache in his bones. Until his head lowered and he turned south and started walking into the woods. Johnny set down his letter, picked up the lantern and followed him. They were more than a hundred yards away from the camp before Johnny called out, "Hey mister. Where you going?"

No response. He kept marching forward, with his arms dangling by his sides and his feet dragging in the dirt.

Johnny chuckled once. The last thing he felt like doing was laughing, but the unsettling way the man walked without acknowledging him made him feel like he had to cut through the tension somehow. "At first I thought you was walking out into the woods for a late night piss, but you're more than far enough from camp for that. So where are you going?"

It was then that Johnny saw where the man was walking. The trees stopped and there lay about fifty feet of rocky terrain and then nothing. The precipice of a high cliff overlooking a rocky ravine with a trickle of a stream that might've been a raging river a thousand years ago lay just beyond the man's hypnotic march.

"What are you doing? Stop!" Johnny called out when he saw where the man's steps led. "Do you understand me? Oh shit. Please tell me you have some English."

Onward he marched, undeterred by the panic in Johnny's voice.

"Shit. Mister, I don't speak Chinese but you got to stop," Johnny pleaded.

As the man unflinchingly walked over the edge and fell limply into the ravine, Johnny dove to try to grab him, but fell short. He landed on his stomach at the edge with his head hanging over the edge. Johnny couldn't get close enough to save the man, but he got close enough to watch him fall.

Johnny thought that seeing the man's impact on the ground would be the worst thing he'd ever see, but what he saw at the bottom of the ravine surrounding the man's broken body far surpassed it. Dozens of bodies with shattered bones, crushed skulls, and limbs twisted in ways they weren't ever meant to littered the ground. It took Johnny nearly a full minute to pick himself up, half paralyzed by the sheer horror of it. When he turned to run back to camp he saw Dan emerge from the treeline.

"Dan! Boy am I glad you saw me head off into the woods and thought to follow. I don't know what the hell is going on here, but one of the workers just walked right off the edge, and it wasn't no accident. He saw the edge coming up, and I told him to stop, but he just went right over." Johnny ran away from the edge and stopped five feet short of Dan. "But it gets worse. I found out where all the workers who've been leaving the job ended up. There's got to be more than a dozen bodies down there!"

No response.

"Dan? What's wrong with you?" Johnny's eyes grew wide with realization. "Oh no, Dan."

As if to kick him while he was down, dozens more from the camp emerged from the woods, each of them with the same dead eyes and heavy feet. By Johnny's estimation, it was every man and woman from the camp and they were all heading for the edge. He pleaded with them to stop and even tried to drag Dan away from the edge, but despite his efforts he kept moving forward at a slow but unstoppable pace. He stood in front of Dan and pressed his shoulder against his chest as if he were trying to barricade a door shut. Johnny's boots dug into the dirt but kept sliding toward the edge.

Johnny pleaded with his words and when he realized what he was talking to was just a shell in which his friend no longer dwelt, he heard a low rumbling, as if the earth itself were an angry wolf. Dozens of bodies shuffled off the edge around Johnny as he looked over his shoulder and saw that he and Dan approached the precipice. The rumble became more than a sound. It grew into something he felt, and finally something he saw.

The gigantic egg-shaped stone rolled through the woods bending trees over as if they were nothing more than blades of tall grass. The moonlight reflected off the symbols in the stone in a color that was both bright and dark at the same time, something that overwhelmed Johnny's senses and caused him to dive out of its path and cover his eyes, partly because he couldn't bear to see his friend stumble over the edge, but also because he felt like if he had to look at those glowing symbols for another second, he'd blind himself. The rumble got louder and more intense until suddenly it was merely an echo reverberating off the surrounding hills. Then it hit the bottom of the ravine with a combined crash of it smashing into the rocks below and the crunch of the bones of the dozens of bodies that now lined the bottom of the ravine.

Johnny opened his eyes and found himself alone and in complete silence. No rumble, no feet dragging on the ground, not even the screams of anyone who hadn't died instantly when they fell and hit the ground. He couldn't even hear the wind or the skittering of animals in the woods. That silence made Johnny think about the horror that God must have felt when He'd made the earth but hadn't yet filled it with creatures of the land.

Then the rumble returned, this time deeper, not coming from the stone, but from the surrounding hills themselves and he saw the cliff's edge begin to fall away with thousands of years of erosion happening all at once. Johnny scrambled to his feet and ran back up the hill through the woods not stopping or even looking back until he reached the camp, climbed up on one of the horses, and rode north until he saw the sun creep over the horizon to his left. It took another three days on horseback to reach a town, and Johnny finally had the presence of mind to consider his next move. Part of him thought that he should go to the only other person who seemed to know to fear the secrets that the stone held, the geologist Bertram Corbitt, but what could either of them do? The earth fell away from the cliff's edge burying the stone and the ones it drove off the edge, and perhaps that was for the best. Rather than risk Bertram coming back and digging the egg-shaped stone out, he thought that if it stayed in the ground where it belonged, the damned thing couldn't do any more harm. Johnny resolved to head back East and start over and not say anything that could send someone back to that Godforsaken stretch of land by the tracks.

He worked a couple of odd jobs to get enough money to resupply and rode out of town a week later, the rising sun at his back the only reassurance he needed to know that he was heading in the right direction. Johnny knew that the earth contained things that made the land a hungry place, but the rising sun at his back and the morning breeze against his face reminded him that it was also a place of healing and new beginnings, and that was what he was determined to find somehow.

It Never Misses

"You remember the rules, Weston?" the man asked, his face worn and beginning to wrinkle, more from long days in the Arizona desert than from years on this earth.

"I remember, Pa," the boy replied. "We been going over it every Sunday night for years."

"You say it this time," the man ordered as he put another log on the fire.

The boy cradled the holstered pistol in his lap. "This here is a Colt 1851 Navy model revolver, sort of like the ones Wild Bill Hickok used, but they ain't like them neither. Those ones had ivory grips and nickel plating. This one's made of a heavier, darker metal...almost like it don't want to be raised up. The grip's made of some dark glassy stone, the geologist who come through town a few years back said it was obsidian, but nobody round here's ever seen anything like it. Six shots before it's got to be reloaded, and the trigger pull is a mite lighter than other revolvers like it."

"That's what you're holding," the man said. "Now what are the rules?"

"We never remove it from its holster unless we intend to fire it," the boy recited. "And we don't so much as aim it at anything we don't intend to kill."

"And the most important one?"

"This weapon ain't to be raised up with any of the seven deadly sins in mind. We don't have it to kill what we hate."

"Why do we have it?"

"To protect what we love."

"And when will it be yours?"

"When I'm older and it's my duty to look after the family." The boy handed the holstered revolver back to his father.

That time wouldn't come for many years, after his pa passed and he got himself married. He and his wife, Elizabeth, raised cattle on the farmstead that had been in Weston's family since his pa was just a boy. Weston's mother lived there with them and helped look after the twin boys who had just turned five scampered around the farm carefree. Elizabeth tried to keep them where they belonged, but Weston didn't mind that too much. There'd be plenty of time for them to work the farm and go to school in Olvido when they were a bit older. For now, they could be free as Adam and Eve was before that Goddamned snake showed up.

Weston hired a few hands during the busy season when he'd need help getting the herd to Olvido, where the cattle would be bought up either for the butcher's block or for other folks to try their hand starting their own farm. He and the two ranch hands, Jed and Caleb woke up before dawn to drink down some coffee and get the cattle up north to Olvido. They arrived well before the midday sun could make the desert heat not just intolerable, but downright dangerous and sold off the cattle at a handsome price. Caleb was young and new to the life of a ranch hand and when Weston saw his eyes go wide when he paid Caleb, he just knew that the money would burn a hole in his pocket.

"Alright, boys. Let's take an hour to buy up any provisions we need, maybe get something to eat. If we leave then, we can get back to the farmstead before the sun goes down," Weston announced, and then he saw Caleb go off in his own direction. Jed stuck around to follow Weston's lead.

"Sometimes a young man's got to lose an honest day's pay in less than an hour at a poker table before he learns to spend what he earns more wisely," Jed mused.

Weston nodded. "I know some who would fire a man for that sort of thing, but one thing I learned from my pa was to lead by example. He said that as long as there was an example to look to, the rest would either sort themselves out or fall by the wayside."

"Your pa was a good man." Jed looked out to the horizon as if he could see into the past when he'd first met Weston's father.

An hour later Weston had been to the general store where he bought some necessary supplies as well as some sweets for his boys and found Jed sitting at the local cantina halfway through a thick ham steak, more indulgent than he'd normally eat, but not a waste of money by any means. He looked down as he stood over the ranch hand and noticed just how old he'd gotten. His hair had gone white and wispy like thin streaks of clouds, and his back had earned a permanent curl making him look nearly two inches shorter than he actually was. Weston thought about the years that Jed had spent working for his father and hoped he'd be able to inspire that kind of loyalty in his own lifetime. He sat down across from the man who used to feel like an uncle to him.

Caleb burst into the cantina with a grin running across his face that reminded Weston of a lit fuse. It was only a matter of time until whatever the cause of his excitement was would come bursting out of him. Weston kicked out a chair from the table he and Jed shared and gestured for Caleb to join them.

"Gentlemen," Caleb beamed. "You're looking at a man who managed to triple his payday in an hour at a poker table! I want to buy you boys a drink. What'll you have Mr. Palmer? Jed?"

"Weston's fine, Caleb," Weston chuckled to himself and realized that he wouldn't be able to talk Caleb out of ordering them a celebratory drink. "A bourbon would be just fine."

Caleb glanced over to Jed.

"I'll have what he's having." Jed nodded back to Weston.

As Caleb went over to the bar with the excitement of a child in his gait, Weston and Jed couldn't help but laugh at his unlikely good luck.

"Sometimes fortune smiles on even the dumbest of decisions," Weston mused.

"That's why we keep making 'em," Jed chuckled. "The hand of fate gives us just enough wins to get us to keep letting our guards down."

The three downed their drinks and hit the trail just a bit later than Weston would have liked, but he didn't mind. The sun would still be hugging the horizon when they got back to the farmstead so long as they made decent time on their return.

They'd made just a few miles out of Olvido and back toward the farmstead when a shot cracked the air and Caleb's horse fell to the ground with a gout of blood pouring from its neck.

"Caleb! You alright?" Weston shouted as his horse reared up and he tried to see where the shot had come from.

"Shit, I think my leg's broke!" Caleb called out.

"Take cover behind your horse's body and see if you can reach your rifle!" Weston cursed the fact that all he had was his father's old pistol. He didn't like the idea of heading into town looking like a small army, so while Caleb and Jed had rifles, he kept his pistol holstered and tucked behind the front of his coat.

Caleb squirmed as best as he could with his broken leg still pinned under the body of his horse. He reached for his rifle when another three shots fired off and he lay still beneath the immense weight of his horse.

"I see them. Five riders coming from the East. They all got rifles!" Jed called out as he lifted his rifle and fired a return shot that sailed past the riders harmlessly.

The riders split off in different directions, the four of them flanking the group on either side and one riding toward Caleb. Jed turned quickly to try to keep track of the four riders who were quickly surrounding them. When he turned all the way around, a rifle shot hit the stock of his rifle, cracking it in half and knocking him off his horse. He tried to pick it back up but his hand throbbed from the impact and he couldn't imagine that he'd be able to grip much of anything with that hand for a while.

The leader of the band of riders stood over Caleb, who opened his eyes and coughed through the spatter of horse blood that had covered his chest and face. His eyes grew wide when he saw the rider was one of the men he'd beaten at poker.

"Did you think we'd let you just ride on out of here when you boasted about all the money you'd made, you stupid son of a bitch?" He raised his pistol and centered it between Caleb's eyes that had grown wide with terror.

A shot rang out and the top half of the rider's head turned into a mist that stained the desert behind him. Weston looked down at the pistol and then up to the shot he'd just made from what seemed like an impossible distance.

"Break off and find a better position!" one of the riders called out. "The farmer's a crack shot. Took Butch's head off from over a hundred yards!"

Weston thought about the impossibility of knowing where they'd be in the darkness if they broke off and the outside chance that they'd make it back to the farmstead before he and Jed, especially if they were carrying Caleb with them. He imagined brutal killers descending on their cozy farmstead that suddenly felt so isolated and unprotected. He raised his pistol and quickly fired another four shots. Before the sound of the shots could finish reverberating off the rocky hills, he heard four bodies fall from their horses to the ground.

"Jesus, Weston! Who taught you how to shoot?" Jed's mouth hung open as he continued to grip his hand.

Weston looked down at his own hand, not believing what he'd seen with his own eyes. "Never mind that. Caleb! You alright?"

"I think so!" Caleb called out from beneath the spray of blood and brain that could have just as easily belonged to the rider or his horse.

They collected the armaments and horses from the dead highwaymen and with Caleb on the back of a horse, they walked the rest of the way back to the farmstead. It was nearly midnight by the time they'd made their return and Elizabeth and the twins waited out front for Weston. When the boys caught sight of their father, they tried to run out to meet him, but Elizabeth held them back when she saw that something had gone wrong. Weston ran ahead and told Elizabeth what had happened and had she and the kids go inside and make ready a space to keep Caleb comfortable until they could get a doctor and a lawman here. As soon as they got him inside, Jed volunteered to ride out to retrieve the help they needed.

Jed made it back to the farmstead with Sheriff Bishop and Doctor Harris from Olvido by dawn. Elizabeth had done what she could to make Caleb comfortable, but she was far from a doctor. Sheriff Bishop asked Caleb a few questions before the doctor gave him a dose of laudanum, so he could work on the broken leg without him crying out and scaring the kids. Then the sheriff asked Weston if he'd step outside to talk.

Sheriff Bishop started smoking his pipe and squinted his eyes as if he were trying to make sense of something. "Both Jed and Caleb tell me that you saved all your lives, made a hell of a shot." As soon as he said that last part, he made a face like the words tasted wrong in his mouth. "No. That ain't right. If what they say is true, then you made a hell of a shot five times in a row in just a few seconds. Is that true?"

"I can't rightly say, sir," Weston replied. "It was dark, and I wasn't exactly counting the paces between where I was and where the bodies are. Am I in some sort of trouble, sheriff?"

"No. Nothing like that. You were attacked and y'all were justified in your response." He blew out a puff of smoke. "I'm just trying to make sense of it, is all. Who taught you to shoot? Were you in the army or something?"

"No, I didn't serve. My pa taught me to shoot. I been hunting a couple of times, but I wouldn't consider myself a marksman or anything."

"I've got to say, Mr. Palmer, the more you tell me, the more impressed I am with how you were able to fend off those riders."

"I don't take any pride in doing violence, sir." Weston looked down at the dirt and imagined it stained with blood. "I just wanted to protect the people I care about."

"You sure did that, Mr. Palmer." The sheriff put away his pipe. "After a cup of coffee, would you feel comfortable riding out to where it happened with me?"

"Whatever I can do to put this all behind us."

Weston and Sheriff Bishop found the bodies just as the sun rose over the crest of one of the surrounding hills and gave a heavenly glow to a truly hellish sight. The sheriff got off his horse and stood at the center of the radius of destruction that Weston had wrought. "Would you say you were standing hereabouts?"

"That looks about right," Weston replied. "I was on horseback though."

Sheriff Bishop looked in disbelief at the distance between where he stood and where the bodies lay. "Jesus. Now by all accounts, you fired off those shots just about as quick as you could get them off. Is that right?"

"That's right, sheriff. I knew that if they broke off into the darkness, they might get back to Elizabeth and the boys before we could. I couldn't let that happen."

The sheriff looked at Weston and then back at the bodies that had begun to stink in the desert sun. "It's just that even an experienced gunman would have a hard time hitting the broad side of a barn at that range, but you managed to hit five bandits on horseback in just a few seconds. It's like some kind of miracle." Sheriff Bishop squinted and wiped his sweaty hands off on his pants.

Weston looked at the death that surrounded him. "I don't know if you could call all this a miracle, sir."

Sheriff Bishop rode out to the bodies and quickly examined each of them. Each of them was shot through the head, their brains were strewn about the dry earth, to be picked at by the creatures of the desert. He rode back to where the dumbfounded Weston waited. "Everything I'm seeing here goes along with what you and the other two you were with told me. I think we're just about done here."

"What's going to happen now?" Weston gestured to the bodies surrounding them.

"I'll have to get somebody to haul these bodies out of here and see if the preacher back in Olvido can read a few words over them when we put them in the ground." Sheriff Bishop hesitated. "I couldn't find anything on their person to tell me who they were, so we ain't gonna keep them cool in a creek while we get word to their people."

"What do I do now?" Weston asked.

Sheriff Bishop considered the question for a moment. "You were justified in all this, so you and I are done with this. I know you're down a ranch hand and a horse, and I'm real sorry about that, but I figure the best thing you can do now is get back to your family and your ranch. Do you need me to ride with you back to the farm?"

"No. I'm fine. Thanks, Sheriff." The two parted ways and Weston tried not to think about the chaos at his back.

When Weston Palmer made it back to the farm, he made sure the boys were out of earshot and then filled in Elizabeth, Caleb, and Jed about what the sheriff said about the matter. Upon hearing some of the details of what happened in the desert, Elizabeth crossed herself and thanked God that her husband and two men she'd come to think of as friends were safe.

Caleb cut in. "I know I won't be able to work while I convalesce, and y'all need another horse. What if we told people about what happened out there. If you could do some target shooting and we'll charge a fee to watch. An uncle of mine once saw Wild Bill Hickock bullseye some playing cards at twenty-five yards and all kinds of folk paid handsomely to see him do it."

"I don't know about all that," Weston cautioned. "I'm no pistolero. I got lucky, is all. Besides, I ain't comfortable advertising what happened."

"No disrespect, Mr. Palmer." Caleb sat up straighter. "But the word is going to get out. Even if the sheriff doesn't talk about it the next time he gets a couple whiskeys in him, think about the men he'll hire to haul those bodies out of there. If even one of them talks about it at a saloon, then everyone in Olvido will know all about it. Y'all might as well get the money to replace the horse because of it…" Caleb hesitated, unsure of whether he was overstepping. "And if some of that money can be put towards the doc making sure I can walk right after this heals up, that'd be mighty fine of you."

Weston thought about all of that. Needing to buy another horse and hire another ranch hand while Caleb recovered would make it tough to keep everyone at the farm well fed over the next few months. He didn't want to raise his pistol with violence in mind again, he didn't see any harm in simple target shooting. He agreed and asked Jed and Caleb see to arranging the exhibition while he got a horse to replace the one the robbers had shot.

It wasn't difficult for Caleb and Jed to bring together a crowd. Caleb displayed his wound like a badge of honor and told tales of how his boss at the ranch rode in like a hero and made five impossible shots faster than most men could even fire a pistol. Jed appreciated the boy's confidence that Weston could repeat the performance, but he wanted to hedge his bets. When he shared the day and time of the exhibition, Jed worded it more like a challenge than a show. He wondered whether Weston had experienced a stroke of luck, divine intervention...or did he discover a talent that he never knew he had? Was this simple ranch owner the greatest gunman the West had ever seen? The only way to find out would be to pay a dollar for a ticket to the show. As luck would have it, a caravan of wagons was set to come through Olvido the day of the exhibition, and between that and the locals who were curious about Weston's abilities, there ended up being a crowd of over fifty. Caleb told the tale of what happened one last time while making a show of hobbling around on his still broken leg and stopping to nail three playing cards to three posts on the edge of town. Then he called out, "I still got a bum leg from the whole ordeal, is there anyone willing to ride out and make sure there ain't nobody behind the posts?

Three men volunteered immediately, eager to be part of the event. When they'd assured the crowd that there wasn't anyone beyond the posts, they stood in the crowd. Weston stepped back twenty-five paces and leveled the pistol aiming at the first playing card. He squeezed the trigger and a chunk of the wooden post flew apart, but the playing card itself remained intact.

"That ain't the same as bullseyeing the playing card," a voice called out. "Anyone could hit a damn post at that range."

"Bullseyeing a playing card ain't the same as taking a man's head off at over two hundred paces neither, but y'all seemed fine with that!" Caleb shouted back.

Weston fired again. This time, he missed the second post completely and the shot hit the rocky ground fifty feet beyond the intended target. The crowd grew restless, and Weston stepped back ten more paces which brought him right to the edge of the crowd. Again, he took aim at the second post. This time, it hit the playing card dead center, but a spark burst from the bullet hole and the unmistakable sound of a ricochet rang out and the entire crowd instinctively dropped.

Weston turned around to see a man standing behind him with a pistol of his own in his hand, aimed at the back of Weston's head. The man stood frozen for a moment until a trickle of blood ran from a hole in his forehead the size of a silver dollar down towards his chin and he fell to the ground.

"That man meant you harm, Mr. Palmer," a man said, raising his hands as if in surrender. "I heard him say that he was going to shoot you after the exhibition, to try to be famous. Be the man who killed the great marksman. I didn't think he would actually try it...otherwise I'd've said something."

Jed clearly saw that Weston was as shocked as everyone else at what happened, but he also knew that admitting the one impressive shot he'd made was an accident would have dozens asking for their dollars back, so he took the liberty of bullshitting them. "Do you see that, folks? Not only did he bullseye the playing card, but he also hit the railroad spike behind it at the perfect angle to shoot the man behind him that meant him harm!"

Once Caleb was able to pull his jaw up off the ground, he caught on quick. "That's right. Palmer here only missed the first two shots to heighten the suspense of it all. He could have hit that playing card any time."

The crowd bought the story and by the time they cleared Weston's would-be assassin out of the crowded thoroughfare, he'd collected enough money to buy two horses and hire a ranch hand for Caleb's entire recovery and then some. It didn't sit well with Weston that they'd made so much money and that someone else was dead behind it, but the man meant to kill him. Didn't that make it okay? He couldn't think of any other way that it could go, but that didn't make it feel any better.

A few weeks later at the farm, Caleb was back on his feet and things had mostly returned to normal, and Weston started to think about what his father had told him about the pistol. "It's not to kill what you hate. It's to protect what you love." Had he done that? Was that what guided his hand to stop those riders from making it to the farm before he could? What about at the exhibition then? All it had done was protect his own hide and help him make money off the whole ordeal.

Weston always wished his father was still alive. Sometimes for the simple joy of saying good morning to him, other times to ask him something he never got around to asking. This time, he wanted to ask him what he meant about the pistol. Did he mean that one in particular, or was that just his own way of telling him how to regard any sort of gun? Where did he get it from? He looked at one of the other pistols that he'd taken off the body of one of the men who meant to rob him. Would these same seemingly miraculous shots happen with a different gun? He'd gone hunting with a rifle before, and he was a decent enough shot, but certainly nothing special. He examined the other pistol and went outside where he set up an empty can on the chopping block next to the pile of chopped logs he'd left out the other night. He stepped back twenty paces and took aim. It took Weston four shots to hit the can, and even then, he'd barely grazed it. Weston repeated the process until he'd gone through an entire box of ammunition and saw that out of every ten shots, he was lucky if he hit the can even once or twice. He decided that it had to be the pistol then and that his father knew something about it that he never passed on to his boy. Weston went inside and asked his mother if they could talk in private. If anyone knew the secret behind the pistol, it would be her.

"What's wrong, Weston?" she asked. Worry added to the creases in her forehead.

"I want to ask you something about Pa, and it might sound strange." He sat down close enough to her that he could speak in hushed tones.

She smiled at the memory of her husband. "Ask your question, and I'll do my best to answer."

"Did he ever tell you anything strange about the pistol he left me? Do you know where he got it?" Weston had several more questions, but he wanted to start a conversation, not an interrogation, so he waited.

She answered with a quick and perhaps rehearsed line. "He got it in the war."

"Right, but that's not the one all the other soldiers got. How was it he came upon that pistol?"

"I can only tell you what he told me." She sighed. "Your father was stationed somewhere in Kentucky and things were looking dire. He told me in a letter that it appeared almost certain that most of his regiment would fall to Confederate troops within the next few weeks. He wanted to find a priest so he could go to confession one last time and leave this world with his soul unburdened. He couldn't find one, but there was a man, looked like a preacher, but your father couldn't rightly tell me what kind. The man agreed to hear him out regardless. Rather than tell him how to repent for the sins he'd confessed, this preacher simply asked him what he feared most. Your father, bless him, told him that his greatest fear was that he might never return to see his loving wife and the baby he'd barely had a chance to get to know before marching off to war."

Weston leaned forward impatiently. "Where does the pistol come into this?"

"It's the strangest thing. This preacher handed it to him and said that the pistol wouldn't let him die if he shot to kill and thought about getting home to us when he did so…" Her voice trailed off. "He took the pistol and the advice. He figured that even if there wasn't anything special about the pistol, it was still just as good as the one he'd been using. But it turned out to be true. He'd make shots that appeared to be out of range, but saved him from onslaughts of enemy troops. It wasn't until one particularly strange occurrence that your father really believed that the pistol was everything that the man who gave it to him said it was."

"What was that?"

"One of his superiors volunteered him and a few others to scout ahead through some particularly treacherous territory. This particular officer must have either had a death wish or wanted to be a hero or something, because when they were offered relief, he refused. After several days of pushing their luck, your father spotted an ambush. When he fired, he hit the soldier who meant to kill your Pa, and when he fell, he dropped his rifle, which hit a rock and went off. The shot from that rifle struck and killed the officer who kept volunteering your father and the others for particularly dangerous tasks. After that, the officer who replaced him wasn't as keen to put his men in harm's way. Your father told me that if it weren't for that shot, he wouldn't have made it home to us."

Normally, Weston wouldn't have believed such an outlandish tale, but after what he'd experienced in the last few weeks, it seemed much more plausible. "Did he ever raise up the pistol again once he got home?"

"Never." Her voice became more stern, and it made Weston feel as if he were a child again. "He always told me that while he'd always consider it a blessing that he was able to make it back home when so many others didn't, the toll it took on his soul was high. This is something he'd never have told you. In fact, I'm not sure he'd want me to tell you, but he always said that he killed far more than his share of men once he got that pistol and that each body he saw fall took away a piece of him. He never wanted that for you."

"Is that why he never told me any of his war stories?" Weston asked, already knowing the answer.

"He'd have been glad you were able to protect your family, but it would break his heart to see you getting in the habit of wielding that pistol."

"Weston Palmer! Get your ass out here," a gravelly voice called out.

Caleb hobbled in with as much haste as he could muster. "Weston. There's some kind of hotshot pistolero calling you out."

Weston stood up from where he sat with his mother and gave her a resigned look. "If I don't go out there, he's going to come in here. If that happens, who knows who'll get caught up in it?"

He stepped out into the evening light that made shadows stretch into those of giants. A man standing in a wide stance with his hands at his waist, tense but ready stood before him with the setting sun at his back.

"We don't need to do this," Weston called out. "Just tell me what you want."

"I want you bleeding out on the ground and that pistol of yours in my holster." The man spat.

Weston looked from side to side and saw how deserted the ranch suddenly looked. "I'll give you the pistol if you agree to leave in peace."

"That ain't how it works, coward!" the man shouted loud enough to make sure everyone at the ranch could hear. "I ain't gonna be the man the greatest gunman in Texas left his pistol to when he retired. I'm gonna be the man who outshot the greatest gunman in Texas and took his pistol off his corpse."

"Listen, friend. I'm trying to give you a choice here. We could both walk away and as far as anyone is concerned, you won."

"I ain't your friend! Draw your pistol or don't, but there ain't no way out of this, except through me."

Weston knew he had no choice but to draw, or die right in front of his family. He focused on aiming low, letting the man limp out of there with a wounded leg and everyone still alive. The man pulled his pistol from the holster and Weston went for his and fired before he could raise it up to a more lethal level.

The bullet grazed the man's thigh just as Weston hoped it would, but gouts of blood sprayed from the wound, staining the ground with the rusty red that Weston had seen far too much of lately.

In seconds, the man lost an amount of blood that would cause most to keel over, but he continued to raise his pistol. Just as the barrel was level with Weston's chest, the man collapsed. As he fell onto the pistol a shot went off under the man's chin taking off his face but leaving the back half of his head attached like a dome growing out of a puddle of gore.

Weston ran to the man as if there were a chance he could even try to save him, and when he knelt over the body and saw exactly what happened, he looked up and saw his boys looking at their father.

"Elizabeth! Get those boys inside now!" he shouted. Weston was never the type to order his wife around, but he had to get his sons away from what happened.

She scooped up the smaller of the two boys under her left arm and grabbed the taller one by the wrist and brought them inside without another word.

Weston checked to see if he'd been covered in any of the blood that stained his farm. When he was satisfied that he hadn't been, he asked Jed and Caleb to see to the man's remains while he saw to his family. He left the pistol in the dirt. Weston didn't want his boys to even see that damned thing again.

Weston went inside and sat down next to his wife. His two boys remained standing, putting them level with each other.

"Did you shoot the bad man?" Francis, the older of the two by all of half an hour asked.

"I did. But he wasn't a bad man," Weston explained. "I don't know if I've ever met a truly evil man. Misguided, greedy, or stupid, perhaps, but given the chance I'd've wanted the man to seek redemption rather than end his days on this earth in violence. Do you understand?"

They stared at him blankly.

"Your daddy didn't want to kill the man. He was just protecting you and your mother," Jed explained.

"But sometimes that isn't enough," Weston continued. "I only wanted to wound him...to scare him and send him on his way, but sometimes it just doesn't work out that way." He wanted to say that the cursed pistol wouldn't let him protect those he loved with anything less than a killing, but his boys weren't ready to comprehend that. Perhaps someday, but not yet.

"Elizabeth. Can you put the boys to bed, and we'll talk after?" Weston asked.

"Come on, boys." she led them to their beds as Weston went outside.

When Weston stood over the body, he realized that the pistol wasn't made for sport, for money, or for anything good. It was meant for one thing; killing. It may have tried to convince him that it was for his family, for his farmstead, for what he cared about, but it wasn't a tool. It was a weapon. Weston told Elizabeth, his mother, and Jed as much of the truth behind the pistol as he could piece together and he told them that he'd be gone for a few days getting rid of the damned thing for good. He kissed his wife and sons goodbye and rode north, first to Olvido to try to destroy the pistol.

He tried to have it melted down so he could use the metal to make something else. Something he could use to build rather than destroy, but the metal of the gun wouldn't melt. He paid the smith extra to make the fires burn hotter, but it didn't so much as soften. Weston resolved to do what was within his power. If he couldn't destroy it, he'd get rid of it.

He rode north for several days until he found a patch of earth deep in a forest that he felt convinced no man had ever laid eyes on before and might never again after he left, and he dug a deep hole in the ground. He tossed the pistol into the hole and filled it back in. Weston pushed his fingers into the soft soil to the knuckle and put a few apple seeds into the dirt. He hoped that a large tree would cover the hole so no one would ever dig up the instrument of evil he hoped he'd banished within the earth forever. As he rode away, he hoped that his efforts wouldn't be in vain, but something about the pistol that never missed seemed so inevitable that he felt defeated already. Sooner or later, it would unearth itself and be found by someone. He prayed that whoever found it would have the sense to put it right back in the earth. His mind was filled with uncertainty but for one thing. He knew that come hell or high water, he'd never hold that pistol again.

The Messenger

"Don't worry. I ain't gonna let you die," Sheriff Dallas Weaver said holding his palm to the bloody groove in his brow. "At least not until you hang in the morning."

Wyatt Porter clutched his thigh as he lay on the ground, unable to even attempt to stand. By all accounts, he should've considered himself lucky. In the war, he'd seen men take a bullet to the thigh and bleed out within minutes, either that or lose the leg to infection in the coming days. He examined his wound and saw that the blood flowed, but didn't spurt out dangerously, and it looked like if Sheriff Weaver had anything to say about it, he wouldn't live long enough for an infection to set in. "If I'm to hang in the morning, why not just let me bleed out?"

"Fair's fair." Weaver knelt down beside the wounded man. "It ain't my place to gun you down in the street like some kind of rabid dog, and while I doubt there'll be any trouble convicting you, it's only right that you stand trial."

"Hell. I nearly shot your eye out, and you're still standing there considering what's right and what ain't." Wyatt groaned.

Sheriff Weaver regarded his blood-stained palm. "You barely grazed me with that derringer. Besides, a few drops of blood don't change right and wrong." When Wyatt rolled onto his side, Weaver rolled gently rolled him onto his back. "You're gonna want to keep that leg up. It'll slow the bleeding."

The doctor came and patched Wyatt up with little difficulty and his trial went as badly as he'd expected. In the chaos of their bank robbery gone wrong, dozens of people had seen him and his crew trying to escape with the money and they'd never quite struck the fear into the hearts of regular folk to the point where your average bystander would hesitate to tell the law what he'd seen. By nightfall the day after the attempted robbery, he found himself in a cell at Sherrif Weaver's station awaiting hanging in the morning.

Wyatt Porter never spent much time considering the morality of his adult life and what it meant for his soul. But once the sheriff left for the night and all he had was the light of a single candle and his own thoughts, he couldn't help but think about it. Ever since he got back from fighting for the Union he'd decided to take what the world owed him after what he'd been through and it worked for a few years, but now he lay in a cell watching a single candle burn down like a timer keeping track of the hours he had left on this earth.

He always thought that a strange peace may come over him when the time came, but that wasn't the case. Part of him wanted to beat on the iron bars and concrete walls until either he broke or they did. Another part of him wanted to break down in tears and beg for forgiveness that he knew he wouldn't get in this lifetime. Mostly he wished that he could just catch his breath and feel peaceful even for just a moment. He'd seen men hang before, some who were friends, some he felt damn well deserved it. What he'd never even thought of was the night before that each of those men had to endure.

Suddenly, his hyperventilating stopped as he heard a footstep that he knew couldn't be there. The sheriff had told him that he was going home to his wife and infant son and that he'd be back in the morning. He didn't seem like the type to say something he didn't mean. Had he forgotten something that forced an early return? No. It couldn't be that. It had to be at least three in the morning. The sheriff and any other right-minded person in the town ought to have been asleep. Wyatt wondered if maybe it were one of his crew who had come back to break him out. He doubted it. They were loyal enough to do a job together but to risk their own hides just to save him would've been asking too much of them. Besides, since this job went so horribly wrong, none of those boys would be returning to this town any time soon.

"Hello," Wyatt called out with an upward inflection of his voice that turned the single word into a question. "Who's there?" He gripped the iron bars and peered out into the darkness. There was no light, save for the single candle in his cell. Whoever was out there was waiting for him in perfect darkness. He picked up the candlestick and stuck it out between the bars, trying to illuminate as much of the small station as he could.

The sound of more footsteps made the floorboards creak and despite the fact that he hadn't felt a breeze all night, a gust of wind blew through the station and extinguished the fragile flame.

The wind stopped as soon as the candle went out and Wyatt heard a long raspy sigh that sounded like someone was standing right in front of him. He flinched and launched himself backward, stumbling over his own boots and falling into the unforgiving concrete wall of his cell.

"Show yourself!" Wyatt commanded although he wasn't sure that he meant it. He thought about who it could be. Had someone who was kin to one of the folks ended up dead in the robbery come to finish him off before the noose could? If so, there wasn't much he could do about it. Even if he weren't locked in a cell, he was unarmed and moving slowly due to his wounded leg. But the same way that waiting for his execution hurt worse than the actual moment would, it was the not knowing that filled Wyatt with more dread than knowing ever could.

Wyatt scrambled for the half-spent book of matches the sheriff had given him in case the candle went out in the night. When he found it he forced himself to slow down. There were only a few matches left and if he broke one in his haste, he'd be trapped in the darkness and whatever lay within it until morning. He struck the match against the abrasive concrete wall and produced a flame.

With the strike of the match, a hideous figure of a broken man stood before him. It was only an instant before Wyatt flinched and dropped the match, but in that moment he saw a man about his age wearing the tattered clothes of a shopkeep who had seen better days and his neck bent at a horrific angle with a bone out of place, creating a bulge beneath the stretched out pale skin.

Wyatt hesitated to light the candle again, but he quickly decided that it was better to see. After he lit the candle and cautiously raised his head to search for the figure, he saw the man sitting in the chair that the new sheriff sat in when he spoke to him. When Wyatt stepped closer, he noticed that he could just barely make out the wood grain of the chair through the form of the man. The man was there and he wasn't there all at once, nearly see-through like a dirty pane of glass.

"Who are you? What are you?" Wyatt stammered.

"My name is Chester Harris...or at least it was," the figure replied matter of factly. "What am I? I think you already know."

"No. It can't be." Wyatt stepped back but was careful not to drop the candle. He only had one matchstick remaining.

"Whatever word you choose to use for it, ghost, specter, spirit, apparition...that's what I am."

Wyatt raised a shaking finger to the side of his own neck. "Your neck...did you...were you--"

"Hanged like you're about to be?" Chester massaged his misshapen neck. "That's right. The only difference is that I didn't deserve it, and from what I saw, you most certainly do."

"Is that why you've come? Are you here to torment me?"

Chester looked at him with a disappointed expression stretched across his pale discolored face. "It ain't all about you, Wyatt. I need something from someone living, and you're the only one who has been able to see me. I don't know if it's because you're so close to joining me on the other side, or that you're having a dark night of the soul right where I had mine, or maybe it's something more than that. Something like fate. Whatever the reason, you're the messenger I've been waiting for."

"If you want me to deliver a message, I'll have to do it when the sheriff asks if I have any last words. He says I'll hang come morning. Did he say the same to you?"

"Him? No. He became sheriff just a year or so ago. At least I think it was a year or so. Time's a funny thing when you've already passed on. Before he was sheriff, it was an older lawman named Shaw. The way he kept order in town was more like a surgeon who would jump straight to amputations before checking to see if they were really necessary. That's how I ended up at the gallows. I bought some goods off a wagon coming through town to sell in my general store. How could I have known that the goods were stolen and that the folks who sold them to me were the highwaymen who'd taken them off some poor travelers they'd killed?"

Chester removed his hand from his broken neck and held it over his heart, mourning himself.

"Is that the message you want me to deliver?" Wyatt asked. "Am I supposed to tell Shaw that he put a good man to death for no damned good reason?"

"No. I imagine he'll die lonesome and unloved, like all men who put power before love, and I don't think even a message from the great hereafter will change his ways." The light dimmed and when the candle glowed brightly again Chester was in the cell next to Wyatt. "I want you to deliver a message to my wife."

Wyatt saw his vulnerability and felt less afraid. "As I said, unless I'm shouting it from within a noose, I won't get the chance."

Chester's head hung low and glanced at the floor where the wind he'd created when he appeared in the station had made a mess of Sheriff Weaver's desk. An iron key lay on the floor, barely obscured by some papers that had blown across the room. Wyatt followed Chester's gaze and when his eyes locked on the keys, he sprung up from his cot and dove onto the floor where he reached between the bars and managed to grab the keys. He stood up and snaked his arm through the bars to unlock the door and scrambled out into the sheriff's station.

Then something struck Wyatt that he hadn't felt in a long time. Was it guilt? No. He'd felt guilty plenty of times. It was a level of empathy that he thought he'd shut out of his heart after seeing and being party to so much death in the war. He felt the sorrow and helplessness that Chester felt, waiting in the cell.

"What do you want me to tell your wife?" Wyatt sighed.

Chester's neck seemed to straighten as he lifted his head. "Tell her I love her and that I'm okay waiting for her. Tell her that I saw her down by the river where I'd proposed to her in her mourning clothes the year after our daughter Isabelle stopped wearing hers. Tell her that when her time comes, to meet me by the river's edge and wherever we end up next, we'll go together."

The longer he talked about his wife and daughter, the less he looked like a corpse and the more he looked like a spirit, and with that change, the empathy that grew within Wyatt's heart increased tenfold. At first, he wanted to climb onto the first horse he saw and ride out of town faster than he'd ever ridden before. By the time Chester finished talking, Wyatt was more than willing to risk being recaptured if it meant he could deliver this message. He stepped back into the cell and shook Chester's hand.

"Her name is Dorothy." As he said her name, his hand went from cold and dead to warm and comforting.

The dull orange glow on the horizon reminded Wyatt of the candle burning down but in reverse. Within an hour, the sun would be up, and stealthily riding out of town would be an impossibility. Luckily, he knew the layout of the small township well since they'd planned their bank robbery using a map of the town that one of his crew had drawn after riding through town to scout for possible threats, points of egress, and places to hide. Finding the general store where Dorothy Harris worked was a simple task. Chester told Wyatt that his wife and daughter lived above the store and that the bedroom on the right side of the hall was that of his beloved. Wyatt estimated that the only difficult part of delivering the message would be convincing her that he was there to deliver a message and not to cause her harm.

Wyatt crept in through an open window and instinctively eyed all of the supplies that would aid him in his escape. He stuffed those thoughts into a leather pouch in the back of his mind. He owed Chester his life and he meant to honor that as best he could. Wyatt looked up the wooden stairs and he could almost hear their creek. Just the same, he had no choice but to ascend the stairs and deliver the message. He took one step at a time and placed his booted foot down gently before allowing it to hold his weight. He repeated the process until he made it three steps from the top of the stairs.

Then a figure rushed out from around the corner and shoved him.

Wyatt crashed down the wooden stairs and hit his body from every conceivable angle as he tumbled down to the main floor of the general store. The final impact with the floor knocked the wind out of him and all he could do was stare at the ceiling as stars danced around the periphery of his vision. Before he could even let out a groan, the heel of a woman's boot pressed down on his right wrist and the cold metal barrels of a double-barreled shotgun jammed against the flesh of his neck.

"You that outlaw meant to hang in the morning?" Her voice came out more harsh and hardened than the angelic presence that Chester described when he talked about his wife. It made sense to Wyatt, but it still took him by surprise.

"Yes ma'am," Wyatt replied in the most even and measured tone he could muster. "Guess I'm lucky you didn't decide to shoot first."

"What are you doing climbing upstairs? Everything you could want is down here, and then I'd have shot you from my window as you left." She jabbed the barrels of her shotgun under Wyatt's chin, reminding him that with the twitch of a finger she could blow his head clean off.

"I ain't here to rob you, ma'am." He pushed himself down into the floor to try and make some room to breathe. "The man who let me out of my cell asked me to deliver a message to you."

"Who?"

Wyatt thought about it and decided that if he told her outright, there'd be even odds between her not believing him, or just shooting him before he could explain himself. "I think it's best if I tell you what he wants told before I say who it was."

She lowered the gun to his chest. "Go on."

He delivered the message, doing his best to repeat what Chester had told him word for word, both to preserve his wording and any subtle meanings that his word choice might provide Dorothy that would have meant little to him. Then he told her the tale of how he'd come to be the messenger for her late husband. "I've got to say, Mrs. Harris, I don't know if it was something to do with being spoken to so plainly by a ghost, or if it was just the way he talked about you, but he loves you and that little girl upstairs with his whole soul."

"He wants me to meet him by the river's edge?" Dorothy's eyes welled up with tears and she loosened her grip on the shotgun.

"When your time comes, that's where he'll be waiting for you." Wyatt nodded, finally at peace.

She wiped away a tear with the sleeve of her dress and lowered the rifle so it was no longer aimed at Wyatt. "What did he say is to be done with you?" she asked, revealing a hint of the Irish accent she'd picked up from her mother.

Wyatt thought about lying. He'd done a hell of a lot worse, but for some reason, misleading Dorothy Harris felt too immoral for him to even consider, consequences be damned. "Truth be told, he didn't say. But if you just let me leave and don't tell anyone you saw me, I'd be obliged."

"You did what Chester asked when you could've just left. It seems to me that we owe you more than that." She gestured to the back door of the general store. "You ride out of town heading north, and I'll tell them you went south." She extended her hand to help him up and he felt the same warmth that he felt from Chester's incorporeal hand earlier.

Wyatt made for the door but turned back at the last moment, sensing that Dorothy wanted to tell him something.

"I don't expect I'll ever see you again," she said. "But I want you to know that I'll always be grateful.

Wyatt rode out of town following the river north, keeping his eye on the river's edge looking for the ethereal glow of a man waiting. He didn't see the glow, but he felt the warmth and knew that he was there.

Hooves

I tell you. The strangest thing I ever seen in this here saloon was when a man who called himself Zachariah darkened the door during one of our nightly poker games, back when he had poker games at the saloon. It was a night not unlike this one, with a chill in the air hinting at the coming of the fall and the night coming earlier and earlier with each passing day. Sat around the poker table were four of our regulars.

There was Maxell St. Germaine, a dude from back East who liked spending his family's money and playing at being the pioneering type. I think he knew better than anyone else that he was full of shit, but he didn't seem to mind. To his right, sat Garrett Wilson, a man who had done just about every job you could imagine in these parts at some time or another during the mere twenty-five years he'd walked this earth. Told me once that he'd even tried his hand at being a lawman. He said he could've been good at it, but it left a bad taste in his mouth. Then there was old Jasper O'Malley. He was an old-timer who spent his days in the creek panning for gold, and spent whatever he found just as quickly on whiskey and cards. Then there was Eli Paulson. He didn't know a damn thing about what cards were likely to be in someone's hand, but he had a talent for pissing people off and getting them to make stupid bets.

I've known some saloon owners who didn't want poker in their joint. They said it slowed the action in a place to a crawl, but in a small saloon like mine, with four tables and a few stools by the bar, it worked out just fine. If one of my four tables had half a dozen guys who kept buying drinks for hours on end, I'd do a good day's business regardless.

I almost forgot. Clem was there too and so was I, except we both had less gray hair back in them days. That was round abouts twenty years ago or more at this point. Back when young men would come into town and order their drinks from Clem rather than me, but they'd call her name out almost like a song. "Clementine." And they'd put as much honey in their voice as they could muster after a long ride on the trail into town. What I'm saying is, I ain't bullshitting you. Hand to God what

I'm about to tell you really happened and if you don't believe me, just ask Clem.

It was a cold night, and we'd just gotten our first dusting of snow from the harsh winter that was to come. Maxwell, Garret, Eli, and Jasper were a few rounds into a poker game. If memory serves, I think Garret was winning, but I could be wrong. Garret's the kind of guy who looks like he's winning even when he ain't. Eli was talking shit, saying that if Garret was as good with women as he was with cards, he'd've given up the game by now. He said it with a sly grin though. That was Eli's game, saying things that'd make you drop your guard. Nobody paid it no mind, save for anyone who didn't know him. He was the sort of guy you'd swear was an unrepentant asshole until you got to know him. After that, you'd know that he'd give you the coat off his back in a blizzard if he considered you a friend. Anyway, Garret didn't fall for it, and he kept his money, at first.

Then he came in.

Man went by the name of Zachariah. Took him for some kind of a preacher or an outlaw at first, dressed as he was, all in black with the shadows keeping pace with his movement, both drawing your attention and not letting you get a full look at him. He bellied up to the bar and ordered a Kentucky bourbon. I couldn't quite place his accent, so I asked him if he was from out that way. He just said that he was from lots of places and he might've picked up a little of the Appalachian drawl along the way. He told me he'd just been dropped off by a wagon coming from back East and intended to spend the night in town before making arrangements for the next leg of his travels.

I think old Jasper was the first to notice him and saw the evidence of the money he might've had. Those black leather boots still had their shine and the tip of each toe had a shiny silver cap that looked like it'd been made from melted down coins. "Does the feller in the black suit want to play some cards while he drinks, or is he just resting his bones?" he asked.

I told him that he ought to ask the man himself, and he did straight away. Zachariah downed the rest of his whiskey and ordered another before he took a seat at the table with the boys. With a voice at once harsh and sweet, like honey whiskey, he thanked them for inviting him to their game and bought a round of drinks for the table. I should've seen trouble coming when he downed the extra drink in one gulp and he chuckled at Maxwell when he sipped at it slowly. He even egged on Eli to pile on the ridicule. "Damn, Maxwell, I don't even need to hear that Yankee accent to know you ain't from whiskey country. All I got to do is watch the way you sip your drink like it's your first."

Normally, Maxwell took it in stride when Eli poked fun at the fact that he came from a well-to-do family in New York, but for some reason, Maxwell took it personal this time. He ordered another drink and downed it in one swallow before raising his bet.

The night crawled on and the men kept drinking, talking, and playing cards. I noticed that the four regulars were putting up more money than they normally would. I didn't pay it no mind at first. It's wasn't any of my business, so long as they had enough left over to pay for their drinks. Normally there weren't any hard feelings in a game between regulars. They'd all be back next time with a determination to win back what they'd lost. Truly the only way the four could suffer a crushing defeat is if some cardshark were passing through just long enough to clean them out and leave forever with their money. Hell, that'd be a loss for me too, since the winnings wouldn't be spent at the bar. I kept an eye out for that, not that I could've done a damn thing about it, but Zachariah, clever as he seemed to be wasn't winning so much as a hand. Either he was a bad card player, or he was just unlucky as all Hell.

None of the boys seemed to mind having Zachariah around. Every joke he cracked split their sides. They followed each suggestion he made without question.

"Oh, Clementine. Get us five steaks so bloody that we'd have to chase them down if they was any rarer." He had a bit of a song in his voice, but Clem always told me that something about it made her feel like a snake was crawling up her arm.

The guys didn't usually eat a full meal while playing cards, but Zachariah insisted on paying for it, so who was I to question it? When Clem got the steaks to the table, I've got to say, I was a little taken aback by the way Zachariah ate his. The way his suit was tailored and cleaned, I'd have thought that he'd tuck a handkerchief into his shirt to keep from making a mess, but I'd have been wrong about that. He cut up the meat into chunks big enough that I'd have choked on them, and he tore into them like a coyote tearing apart a jackrabbit. He was right when he said he liked his steak bloody, and I swear, if he wasn't clean-shaven, his beard would have been stained red from it.

There followed a few more hands, and I noticed that my regulars weren't playing like they was friends anymore. Sure, they always got in their jabs, sometimes just for a laugh or sometimes to trick a man into making a stupid bet. And yeah, sometimes it got out of hand, particularly when one or more of them's had a drink too many, but the worst it ever got was old Jasper would sit out the next few games and claim it was because he'd been spending more time in the creek panning for gold. Then he'd come back a week or two later like nothing ever happened. This didn't feel like that. You know that feeling in a room when you just know something bad's going to happen? I've been tending bar for the better part of thirty years and I've seen things go bad more than once...Anyway, that's the feeling I got.

Next thing you know, old Jasper called Garret's bluff and came out on top with three aces in his hand. Trouble was, there shouldn't have been three aces left in the deck. I wasn't sure at first, but Clem told me that from what she'd seen when she brought them their drinks, those cards had already been played. Anyway, Garret took that personally.

"You can't have had that hand," Garret shouted. "With what's been played so far, there ain't that many aces left in the deck."

"Yer the one cheatin!" Jasper countered. "How would you know how many aces should be left if you weren't cheating?"

"Paying attention ain't cheating." Garret slammed his fist on the table. "Just because you're too much of a God damned drunk to do it yourself don't make it cheating."

Zachariah stood up with a movement both lightning-fast and so smooth that the two men hardly noticed him until he positioned himself between them. "Easy, boys. The night is young. You'll have plenty of time to win that money back, Garret. That is, if you keep on playing. Can't win your money back from Jasper if he leaves the game with a broken nose."

"Prove that you ain't cheating," Garret demanded.

"Gentlemen, we can solve this quite simply. We can check the discarded cards and see if the aces have been played," Zachariah offered. "That is if everyone here agrees to it."

Jasper was the first to respond. "I'm fine with it. Go ahead and prove I ain't cheatin."

"We'll see about that," Garret growled.

"Well shit. Go ahead and check so they can get back to losing their money to me." Eli added, unable to hold back an opportunity to twist the knife a bit.

"I suppose if it will diffuse the situation, I'm game," Maxwell added.

Zachariah slowly went through the deck, thoughtfully making sure each man could see every card as he went. When all was said and done, the aces Garret expected to see weren't there and it looked like old Jasper was right.

"Well shit," Garret's jaw dropped open. "I could've sworn some of those cards had already been played."

"I don't mean to offend," Zachariah placed a hand on Garret's shoulder like a father trying to console a confused child. "But you have been drinking. What's more likely, that old Jasper here has been a master card shark this whole time, or that you simply counted wrong?"

That seemed to placate Garret enough for him to sit down and pick his cards back up.

Now you might think that Zachariah diffused the situation there, but you'd have been wrong. All he did was light a longer fuse. The men kept throwing back drinks and playing like they were betting lives rather than a few dollars. Again, there was just an air that things weren't going to end well. More than a few of my regulars who weren't card players cleared out of the place, and I can't say I blamed them.

As the pot deepened and the evening turned into night, Eli's verbal sparring, once playful, had turned downright venomous. When Jasper put forth a bet that was a mite more conservative than others that'd been placed that night, Eli had some choice words for old Jasper. He put on a bad Irish accent and said, "Oh. Is that your whole bet? Sure you don't want to raise me a couple potatoes, or can you afford it?"

Now I swear to you that Jasper was the gentlest old man you ever saw. The closest thing anyone had ever seen to an act of malice from him was when he raised up a pickaxe to break some gold out of the earth, but he shot out of his seat like he'd been shot out of a cannon and lunged at poor Eli with his steak knife and slashed his old friend from ear to ear. Garret and Maxwell each grabbed an arm and dragged him back from the table, but they needn't have. The second he cut Eli, Jasper dropped the knife. It was like all the rage that had built up in him over the course of the night just, went away. I don't mean that as he let it out when he killed him. It was more like the anger that consumed him just disappeared like it weren't even his in the first place.

Before Jasper could quit stammering and say something, Zachariah scooped up his winnings and excused himself, saying that these boys weren't the type of folk he liked to keep company with, and just as quick as he'd come in, he was out the door.

"Y'all, what the Hell happened to us tonight?" Jasper asked himself just as much as he asked the rest of us. "The way we was acting tonight...that ain't us."

Garret was always the type to keep his cool, even in a tough spot. He was the first one to say what they were all thinking. "What made tonight different than any other? Zachariah. Who stood to gain from us going at one another like we did? Zachariah. Who walked away with our money?"

They all glanced at the door.

"I don't know how he did it, but he brought out the worst in all of us." Garret pulled his pistol from the holster on his hip. "I think we ought to give him a piece of our minds for what he did."

Having just watched Zachariah work his magic on these boys, I worried that maybe he'd talk his way out of it, but they were wise to it at that point. I saw the way that Garret held his pistol with his muscles loose so he could draw fast and the hammer already pulled back. There wasn't going to be much talking. I told them what he said to me about being dropped off by a wagon and that he had to be on foot. Clem even confirmed it, saying that she didn't see a horse tied off outside that could've belonged to him.

"Come on, y'all," Garret called out. "We can catch him before he gets to the stables, and he'll be easy to track in the snow."

I asked Clem to mind the bar and went with them. If I hadn't I wouldn't have believed what I saw. We stepped out into the snow and there wasn't a single set of footprints in the snow, only a set of what looked like the impossibly large hoofprints of some giant goat. I know what you're thinking. Hoofprints too big to be a goat. It's got to be a horse. I tell you here and now that they were goat hooves, longer and more pointed than the round prints left by horses. That's when we knew exactly who had been sitting at the bar with us, bringing out our worst inclinations for violence and hate. Garret tried to follow the prints, but they disappeared at the edge of town, and I've got to tell you, I'm glad they weren't able to track him down. A card game left one of our own dead. I can't imagine what would've happened had we confronted him. All I can say is that I hope he never darkens my door again, and I'll be wise to keep watch for a mysterious stranger descending on this place like some kind of plague.

Among the Willows

Loretta Hammond understood the language of fear. She didn't speak it, of course, but she saw it in the averted eyes and cautious posture of everyone she crossed paths with. Even when a man walked her from her home to somewhere in the township, he monitored his every movement as if his life depended on it. All because of who her father was.

At first, he wasn't much more than a businessman with good timing. He arrived in the township of Whisper Creek, Nebraska right when it went from being a camp to a real town and he was able to buy out shops in the marketplace run by men who knew they weren't cut out for what Whisper Creek was becoming. He grew in power and influence as he bought up swaths of land that he knew would be peopled within a year or so. But it wasn't until he signed his name as one of the founding members of the township's first proper bank that he truly cemented himself as the little king of the little hill that Whisper Creek, Nebraska sat upon.

When Mr. Hammond called on his wife and only daughter to join him from their former life in Denver, Loretta Hammond suddenly realized the power that her father wielded and why he chose this small town over the bigger city where he'd started his business. There he was just one of the dozens of such men. In the emerging township, he could bend the entire community to his will.

That kind of power only makes it easier to gain more, and that's exactly what Mr. Hammond did. If someone crossed him...hell, they didn't even have to do that. If they displeased him or stood in the way of what he wanted, they didn't last long. If he wanted someone to hang, they hung. Either that, or they cut their losses, packed up what they could, and escaped the town on a wagon under the cover of darkness. After they left and a little time passed, Mr. Hammond would simply purchase the property from the bank, and as one of the founding members of the bank, you can bet he got a good deal.

Loretta heard other girls wishing they'd been born princesses, but she knew that a title like that could just mean being born the spawn of a monster and being feared like one just the same. When she was little, the other girls in the township never contradicted her when they played together. She learned not to compliment another girl's doll because if she did, that girl would try to give it to her as a gift within the next few days. When she got a little older and wanted the attention of some of the boys in town, they'd never make their possible affections known to her. Eventually, she approached a boy she'd seen at the one hotel in town, the manager's son. Loretta told him she thought he was handsome and wondered if he'd ever get around to calling on her...The boy's response wasn't what she'd hoped.

"Miss Hammond! Please don't tell nobody we talked like this," he pleaded.

"Why?"

"Oh my God," he muttered through his hyperventilating. "I feel like my neck is in a noose."

"What's the matter? You don't like me?"

"I never said that!" He held up his hands defensively.

"Then what is it?" Loretta's hopeful smile sunk into a pout.

"You promise not to repeat a word of what I'm gonna say to you?"

Loretta saw that agreeing to the promise was the only way he'd open up. "I promise. Now, what in the world is so damn terrifying about calling on a girl like me?"

"It ain't you, Miss Hammond. It's your daddy. If I turned you down, then he'd have me hang for breaking his only daughter's heart. If I were to call on you, I'd feel his eyes on us whenever we were out together. There'd be a gun to my head whenever I went to hold your hand or...try for a kiss." He hung his head low, feeling like he'd signed his own death warrant. "For my sake, I hope you ain't mad, and for your sake, I hope you understand."

"I understand," she replied.

"I must seem like quite a coward to you now." His expression was an ambivalent cross between relief and heartbreak.

The frustration and anger at her supposedly fortunate circumstances threatened to rise to the forefront of her mind, but unlike her father, she decided to react with empathy rather than wrath. "You ain't a coward. You're the only one in all of Whisper Creek with the courage to tell me the truth." She kissed him on the cheek.

Over the weeks and months of her adolescence, Loretta tested the effect that the fear her family inspired and how it made her feel. She walked out of the general store with some sweets that she hadn't paid for and the shopkeeper didn't so much as acknowledge her. That could be since her father technically owned the general store, but it could be that invisible noose that everyone she encountered instinctively felt. She ate the sweets, but they left a bad taste in her mouth, not because there was anything wrong with them, but because of how she acquired them. They tasted like fear, and it tasted like ash in her mouth. While the power she inherited soured the small pleasures of life for her, it made her father drunk. The man never touched a drop of alcohol outside of champagne when it was expected of him at high society social gatherings, but he was just as much a drunk as the men who hurled their guts onto the dirt behind one of the half dozen saloons that had cropped up in town over the years. He was just as much an addict as her mother, who numbed herself with laudanum whether she had a headache or not. His drug was power, and it was just as dangerous as anything else, maybe more.

Loretta looked to the horizon of her life and saw womanhood and all that the world would expect of her as it came. It made her think about her mother. She hadn't been much older than Loretta's sixteen years when she met the man who would become her husband. Did she see the monster that dwelt within him when they first met? Did she go through courtship and into marriage knowing the type of man he would become? And if she did see it, did she decide it was worth it for a life of wealth and comfort? When Loretta got a little older would she have to make the same decision? Was it even a decision, or a fate that would be thrust upon her? Loretta Hammond didn't know what she wanted out of her life, but she damn sure knew what she didn't want. She didn't want to be like her mother and she sure as hell didn't want to end up like her father. Looking out on that horizon she searched for a way to escape the snare she felt trapped within. An image of a rabbit caught in a trap chewing off its own leg to get free flashed through her mind. That's what she'd have to do. Sever herself from this place, these people, and start over somewhere else. Somewhere where she could become who she wanted to become rather than being the extension of something horrible.

Loretta set to the task of figuring out how to start over and build a life of her own. Whisper Creek wasn't a town that pretended piety, and she'd seen where girls who come into town without means end up. If she was going to build a new life, there'd be more to it than just finding a way to get far away. She'd also need to squirrel away some money and do what she could to ensure her father wouldn't send anyone to find her and bring her home. What she needed was to burn a bridge or two.

She made a hiding place beneath a floorboard under the dresser in her bedroom, and she started keeping things down there. First, a map where she marked a few cities far enough away that she could forge a new identity and nobody would be the wiser. Loretta looked at San Francisco, and New Orleans, as two such places and imagined how different her life would be depending on which she chose. Suddenly her very prescribed life grew larger and more full of glorious uncertainty.

Loretta was hopeful but she wasn't stupid. She knew that traveling alone was dangerous for a young woman, so the next thing she packed away in her hiding place was a hunting knife. A blade small enough to conceal beneath her skirts, but big enough to intimidate someone if needed.

Once she had a destination and a means not to be killed on the road, she began thinking about the necessities that would get her to wherever she decided to go. Loretta would stash away money, a few cents at a time at first, and then a dollar every so often. She bought a bag more suited to a military scout than to a young lady and kept all of her hidden belongings in it. It didn't suit her, but she imagined that when she left Whisper Creek, Nebraska, she'd have to do so under cover of darkness and she wouldn't be able to bring several bags of luggage.

Within a few months, she had two bags beneath the floorboards with enough clothes, money, and supplies to get her started, but when she thought about what life would be once she arrived at her destination she said to herself, "It's not nearly enough." In order to go to a whole new place, and become a whole new person, she'd need the kind of money that would let her pay off anyone who might ask too many questions. Loretta thought and realized the answer was sitting right in front of her. If someone were to rob her father's businesses he'd be too concerned with that to spend much time searching for her. She'd burn a bridge and get what she needed at the same time.

The area certainly had no shortage of road agents, guns for hire, and other outlaws, but for Loretta, the hard part was finding a band of bandits that she felt could do the job and not just take her cut and leave her to die, or worse. Consorting with the type of folk willing to steal a large sum of money from a powerful man would be a dangerous task, but it was one of many risks Loretta decided she needed to take.

Loretta began asking father if she could join him on business trips to Denver, not that she wanted anything to do with his business dealings, but because she wanted to become more well versed in traveling, and people outside the fiefdom that he'd created and kept her in for most of her life. If she was going to enlist the help of a band of outlaws, she certainly wasn't going to find them in or around Whisper Creek. It took her six months and several trips to Denver, Dodge City, and a few other larger towns where Mr. Hammond had business dealings, but she found a small clutch of men who seemed smart and rugged enough to do what she needed them too, but not so calculating and ruthless that she'd have to spend every moment worrying about preserving her own hide. Their ring leader, as much as they had one, was an old timer with a hitch in his step from an old wound who went by the name of Lucky. He claimed that he took on the name because he was a distant relation of British nobility and he wanted to keep his lineage out of his business. She remembered Morgan, one of the ruffians

Lucky kept company with, tried telling her that it was because he was set to hang one morning after he'd been caught by a local sheriff and he somehow slipped through the noose and dodged a hail of gunfire as he made his escape. Loretta doubted both stories, but who was she to blame someone for reinventing his past, whatever it may be? She arranged that they meet in the lobby of the large hotel where she stayed where she would then lead them to a second room she'd reserved without her father knowing to have a private place to talk. At first, Loretta thought that it would've been more difficult to make these arrangements and get the five men into the hotel unnoticed, but after staying in the Grand Union Hotel a few times, she'd come to notice that the clerk who worked the night shift had a bad habit of napping on the job. In the quiet hours when most of the city slept, Lucky and his compatriots filed into the room.

Lucky announced to the men who flanked him on either side, "Boys. This is Miss Loretta, and she's got an idea for a job that could be mutually beneficial for us and for her." Then he turned to Loretta. "Miss.

Loretta. This here's my crew. Anton, Morgan, and Joaquin. Anything you can tell me, you can tell them. So let's talk about the job."

Morgan, Anton, and Joaquin sat down regarding Loretta with curiosity rather than suspicion. Normally they wouldn't have trusted her so quickly, but Lucky vouched for her and that was enough for each of them. Lucky had always been a good judge of character and could smell a lie just as well as any lawman ever could.

Loretta felt apprehensive but sat down just the same. "Lucky. You were very tactful in referring to me by my given name only, and I appreciate that. Do the rest of you know who I am?"

Anton, who looked like he couldn't have been more than twenty years old, with a look that told Loretta that he'd spent part of his life oppressed by men like her father, perhaps born into slavery and liberated, by some means as a young man, nodded knowingly. Morgan and Joaquin looked to Lucky for an answer.

Lucky replied to their wordless question. "This here's Loretta Hammond. Daughter of Bartholomew Hammond. The man that practically owns Whisper Creek, Nebraska."

Loretta noticed the change in their expression from one of mild amusement to one more grave. "That's exactly what I'm looking to get away from, and that's exactly why y'all are going to help me."

Lucky knew that the boys in his group wouldn't truly be interested until they knew what they stood to gain. "That's right boys. She's looking to get out, to start fresh. Who among us hasn't done that, or at least wanted to before? The difference is, Miss Loretta here has a plan for doing so that can make us all rich men."

"How rich we talking?" Morgan asked.

"Let me put it this way," Loretta started, trying to match the gruffness of their voices without trying too hard. "Even a king's ransom split five ways is still a hell of a lot of money."

Morgan grinned greedily. "Is that the split? Five ways even?"

Lucky noticed the discomfort manifesting in Loretta in the form of a downward glance and a hesitation of her response. He cut in. "We got a good deal here, Morgan. Don't get greedy or try any bullshit. Miss Loretta's taking half and we're going to split our half like usual." He glanced at Anton and Joaquin. "With that split, we're still set to make as much in a week as we're likely to the rest of the year, so listen to her plan."

Loretta collected herself and continued, "As you all know, my father owns most of the property and businesses in Whisper Creek, Nebraska. Just about nobody lives or works there without paying their percentage to him each month. The thing is, everyone in town is so damn scared of him that he doesn't need much in the way of guarding the money when they're getting it back to the safe." She did her best to match Morgan's greedy smirk. "That's where y'all come in."

Anton chimed in. "So is that the plan? Wait until payday and then take the bank?"

"It's not as simple as that," Loretta explained. "The bank is heavily guarded and besides, that's not where most of the money will be."

"The more you tell us, the better we can do for you, Miss Loretta," Lucky said with the gentle push that the best of her tutors had. "Lay all the cards on the table and then we'll put in our two cents."

Loretta understood that the plan would be more of a collaboration than simply having Lucky and his men follow her plan. It made sense to her. While she thought that her plan was good, she was hardly well-practiced at such things. "While he has grown careless over the years with keeping his courier well guarded as he collects payments, his caution regarding bank robberies has remained. That's why the majority of his money isn't in the bank. It's in a safe in the house. My plan involves you simply waiting in ambush and...subduing the courier when he opens the safe, taking its contents, and then escorting me from the town under the guise of using me as a hostage. After we've made it several days from Whisper Creek, we can divide the spoils of our labors and go our separate ways."

Lucky considered her plan. It was better thought out than he guessed it would be, but it didn't account for the chaos and unexpected variables that inevitably came up in any job. He considered his years of experience and what he knew about the men he was working with. "That all sounds good, Miss Loretta. There are just a few wrinkles we've got to iron out before we're set."

"You're the professional, Lucky. What details have I missed?" Loretta asked.

"Ain't so much that you missed. Just a few things ain't been accounted for. Things that may complicate things. For example, if the safe is in your parents' house, what are we to do with them? What if your old man puts up a fight?"

Loretta hadn't thought of that. Her father always seemed so invulnerable that it almost seemed shocking that a revolver, costing less than ten dollars could take him from this world and his monument of wealth and power. "My mother will be half asleep from laudanum and my father...he may be a cruel man, I may never want to see him again, but he's still my father. I don't want him killed."

"You got that, boys?" Lucky gave the three men a stern glare. "If Mr. Hammond doesn't make it to the other side of this in one piece, the one who killed him will lose more than their share of the money." He hadn't had to follow through on a threat like that in years and part of him wondered if he still had it in him. Lucky silently prayed that it wouldn't come to that. Morgan was a bit of a loose cannon, but Anton and Joaquin had quickly learned that following Lucky's orders tended to lead to jobs going smoothly and everybody getting paid. Lucky told himself to make sure that Morgan's tasks were ones suited to him and they'd be alright. Every toolbox needed a hammer and that was Morgan.

Loretta and Lucky ironed out several other complications, and when she was confident that despite the danger and uncertainty that lay ahead, they'd done what they could to prepare. They marked the date that payments were due and went their separate ways to prepare for the storm to come.

The two weeks between meeting with Lucky and the day their plan would come to fruition passed agonizingly slow for Loretta. She tried to busy herself both with practical preparations and aspirational dreams of what life could be after the chaos passed. There'd be so many people she'd likely never see again, and she imagined that after a few years passed, they may not even recognize her.

When the night before Lucky and his men were to come and help her change her life forever came, Loretta tried to get to sleep early, but sleep wouldn't come. She stared at the ceiling, rolled over in her bed, and thought about everything and nothing at the same time. She read several dozen pages of her well worn copy of Jane Eyre which she'd already read cover to cover more times than she could count. Taken from the tension of her life and transported into the pages of her favorite book, a restful mind finally came and she slept with the pages pressed against her chest.

Loretta spent the morning that would change her life split between going through her normal routine and keeping her eyes fixed on her pocket watch so she could make sure to be home by noon when Lucky and the others were set to swoop in, seemingly from nowhere. She wore a dress that looked like something she'd wear any day, but she made sure to wear boots with a lower heel that would allow her to move quickly and through rough terrain. Her instructions to Anton and Joaquin included ransacking the house and making sure to grab certain pieces of jewelry and clothing from her things, both so she would have clothing to wear, and so she could barter them as she traveled. Going through the house and taking what was worth taking would also go a long way in making it look like a band of outlaws looking to rob a rich man's house just happened to get lucky and catch him with the safe wide open rather than something planned.

When she saw her father's courier, a man named O'Malley approaching the house, she stood where she told Lucky she'd be when she drew a map of the house. As Loretta watched O'Malley walking into the house with the bags of money gripped tightly in his left hand, she prepared to act surprised when Lucky and the others burst in, but it turned out she didn't need to fake it. She'd known for weeks that they'd be coming, but what took her by surprise was the ferocity that they had as they grabbed O'Malley by the back of his shirt and shoved him head first into the safe he'd just opened, hard enough to make blood pour down his forehead, but not so hard as to render him unconscious. Anton held open a bag which he forced O'Malley to fill with the contents of the safe that would be useful to them. First the money, then the gold.

When all that remained in the safe were deeds to land and a .44 Derringer in the back, Anton ordered, "Alright. I'm gonna need you to pick up that pistol real slow, and lower it into the bag. Any quick moves'll be your last, so don't try nothing."

O'Malley followed Anton's orders to the letter. Even if he could fire the Derringer fast enough, he only had two shots and there were four of them, and one of them had taken hold of Loretta.

Lucky took hold of Loretta and held a gun on her. Of course, back when they'd planned all this out, he assured her that he always kept one chamber empty and that there would be no way it could fire by accident. As Lucky pulled Loretta from room to room, taking what was both valuable and easy to carry, she noticed that Morgan was still outside standing guard as they had planned. If he fired one shot, it meant they had company. If he fired twice, it was the signal that there was trouble and they should find a good spot to return fire from concealment. So far he hadn't had to fire at all.

Almost as if thinking about Morgan set it off, his pistol fired once and everyone's attention turned to the front of the house. Lucky looked out the window and Bartholemew Hammond approached the house steadily, his hands raised to ward off another shot from Morgan.

"The first one was a warning shot. I'm putting the next one in your gut," Morgan shouted at the still approaching Bartholemew.

"I assure you, if you wound me, it will be the stupidest thing you've ever done, and judging by where you're standing right now, I imagine there's some competition for that title." Bartholomew Hammond walked forward with a sense of cautious invincibility.

"And I assure you," Morgan spat back, mocking Hammonds words, "that if you get any closer I'll put one in your kneecap."

"Interesting." Hammond grinned. "Thus far, you've threatened a shot to the gut, and another to the knee. It sounds like you've been ordered to leave me alive. That's the one smart bit of caution whoever hired you took."

Lucky and the others saw the stalemate Morgan had found himself in and burst out the front door with a gun to Loretta's head and bags filled with money and other valuables. Seeing his daughter with them caused him to finally stop inching forward.

"The only way you're going to see this girl alive again is if we get out of here safe. Once we make it out of here and nobody's following us, we'll drop her off a mile or so outside some township between here and California." Lucky raised a grin beneath the bandana he wore as a mask.

"I'm sure she'll send word once she gets there, and you can send for her."

"And if I refuse?" Hammond asked with a tone of playful curiosity more so than concern.

Lucky jammed the barrel of the gun into Loretta's back. "Then I guess you can pick up what's left of her off the ground right here."

"Don't be foolish." Hammond laughed. "That girl is the only reason you're still alive."

"You're bluffing," Joaquin called. "The only gunmen in town are at the bank."

Lucky wordlessly glared at Joaquin for giving up what they knew about the guards at the bank. He'd reprimand him for it once they got clear of town, but for the time being, the look Lucky game him would have to do.

"I may not have my own personal guard, but I own this town and everyone in it," Bartholemew Hammond said just loud enough for them to hear, and then called out loud enough for everyone to hear. "People of

Whisper Creek! Two hundred dollars for the heads of these men. That's two hundred each, and I'll double it if you get my daughter back alive!"

People ranging from barbers and shopkeepers, to simple farmers poured out of homes and businesses, some armed with hunting rifles, others with whatever farming tools they had on hand. Lucky hoisted Loretta onto his horse and took off on the road north out of town so he and his group could make as much distance between them and the impromptu mob chasing them down as they could before they mounted horses of their own.

They raced out of Whisper Creek as fast as they could, with the weight of their loot slowing the horses down. Lucky assured the group that if they could get off the road before they got the guards from the bank mounted on horseback they'd be alright, reasoning that they were likely the only decent shots in town. About five miles out of town they couldn't see their pursuers, but they could hear pistol shots and hurried hoofbeats on the ground.

Joaquin looked to a patch of forest to their right, and turned to the group. "It would be harder to track us."

Lucky gestured to the woods. "Miss Loretta. Are those woods as deep as they look?"

Loretta sat up straighter, trying to feel less like a hostage and more like an accomplice. "I think so. People from Whisper Creek don't go into these woods much for hunting and whatnot. They say there ain't nothing worth having in these woods."

"Even better," Morgan added. "They won't know the land more than anyone else."

Lucky thought for a moment about the general direction of the nearest cities. "It's northeast into the woods. If we get through there we can make our way to Sioux City and from there we can get anywhere else."

"Better than them running us down on the well worn trail." Anton sighed.

Loretta thought about making it to the Mississippi River and making her way down to New Orleans like she'd planned. "That sounds reasonable."

With her final approval, the men took the four horses into the forest and once they lost sight of the trail, they slowed their pace enough that it would be difficult for their pursuers to hear them. Although it was barely evening, the sun began to sink low in the sky.

"Come on, y'all," Lucky grunted. "We need to make some distance between us and them and set up camp before we lose the light completely."

The group made camp at the base of a ravine between a high cliff to the southwest and a creek that flowed southeast. Joaquin, the most skilled at navigating wilderness among the group, reasoned that the cliffs would block the view of their campfire and the horses could drink from the stream.

Despite the fact that nearly everything had gone according to plan, save for the impromptu militia of townsfolk after them, Loretta still wasn't sure if she completely trusted Lucky and his men. After all, what was to stop them from simply taking her share of the money and leaving her out there? For that reason, she insisted that they split up the money into bags that each of them would carry. Of course, she didn't tell them it was because she didn't trust them. She said it was just in case they got separated in the forest. Although they saw through her facade and knew exactly why she was making the suggestion, the men went along with it.

"Hell. I don't mind," Morgan said. "If it means I don't have to carry someone else's share of what we got, I'm fine with it."

Lucky read the apprehension written on Loretta's face and handed her the .44 Derringer they got from the back of the safe. "A purse gun like this one seems like something you may want to have after we go our separate ways and you're on your own. Do you know how to use one?"

Loretta held it carefully. She hesitated to reply truthfully. "I've seen one used a few times, but no. Nobody ever showed me how."

"Anton's the best shot out of us. He can show you how to load it, shoot it, and keep it clean and working reliably," Lucky offered.

Loretta thought about the idea and it surprised her that the first thing she thought was that her father wouldn't allow it for so many reasons. She had to remind herself that those days were over, she'd be reinventing herself as an heiress, perhaps from another country, if she could fake the accent and rewrite her story. That started now, with saying yes.

"Come on over here Miss Loretta," Anton called. "It's best we stand clear of the others while I show you how this works…just to be safe."

"Okay, Anton. What do I need to know first?" She felt strange speaking to him alone, and in such an informal fashion, but out there in the forest, without the arbitrary rules and expectations placed upon the natural world by humans, it didn't seem to matter. She wondered if it ever really did.

"The first thing you need to know is to always keep it pointed down unless you're aiming it at something," Anton explained as he guided her hand down. "If you're careful and keep your finger off the trigger until you're ready to shoot, it should be fine, but you don't want to roll those dice if there's even a chance."

"Certainly not." Loretta agreed and then mused. "It's almost hard to believe that something so small could be so deadly."

"That's the other thing you need to know. Just because it's small and folks call it a purse gun, don't mean it's not just as deadly as anything that me or the others are carrying. The only difference is that we get five or six shots instead of the two shots you get, and the barrel of yours is shorter."

"What does that mean?" Loretta asked.

"It just means that since your pistol's shorter," Anton traced a fingertip along the top of the barrel. "It's less accurate at a distance. Basically, it means that this is meant for protecting yourself from close range."

Loretta asked, "What would be considered close range?"

Anton thought about it. He'd never had any formal schooling so he couldn't accurately give her a true measurement. "Fifteen or twenty paces," he estimated and then stepped back a generous fifteen steps. "If someone's further away than this, even an experienced marksman might miss with a short-barreled pistol like that."

She digested the information and committed the distance to memory. "Okay. Show me the rest. How do I fire it accurately? How do I reload it after my two shots are spent? Will it require any maintenance to remain accurate and reliable?"

Anton showed Loretta the workings of the Derringer while the rest of the men sat around the fire, tending to it to keep the flame warm and the smoke low so as not to advertise their location to anyone who may still be searching for them.

"You really think that's such a bright idea?" Morgan gestured to Anton and Loretta while maintaining eye contact with Lucky.

"What's the matter? Did you want the purse gun for yourself?" Lucky chuckled.

"That ain't it." Morgan scowled defensively. "I just don't want to get shot by one. That's all."

Joaquin's eyes darted between the two men and hoped that it wouldn't come to blows. Out of the crew, Joaquin had been with Lucky the longest and had seen him brutally beat men over challenging his leadership. It wasn't something Lucky ever threatened, but when it came down to it, he was more than able to hold his own against a younger, stronger opponent.

Lucky considered how to prevent their disagreement over whether Loretta should be armed or not from coming to blows. Morgan had good instincts and he was indispensable in a fight. Lucky would hate to lose him if worse came to worst. "She'd be foolish to turn that gun on any of us unless her life depended on it," he reasoned. "Even if she could pull and fire a shot faster than us, she's got two shots and there's four of us."

"I guess that makes sense," Morgan grumbled. "Don't mean I have to like it."

"That's fine, Morgan," Lucky said. "I don't mind you keeping a keen lookout for her or anyone else that could mean us harm. That's how you help keep the crew protected." Lucky hoped that the compliment would placate Morgan enough that he wouldn't have to sleep with one eye open until he cooled down. As was often the case, Lucky offered to keep watch first, to ensure that his men were well rested and that he could tend to the fire and keep an ear to the ground for anything that might approach their camp, whether it be wolves or someone from Whisper Creek looking to collect their bounty.

The fire died down and became a bed of glowing embers that would keep their camp warm enough through the night. Loretta felt more secure with her new pistol close at hand, but she still made sure to sleep closer to the horses than anyone else. That way nobody could leave without her, or if she were threatened, she could fire her two shots and make a break for the horses.

Loretta lost herself in the feeling of being between two lives as sleep encroached on her dulling senses and she managed to fall asleep on the meager horse blanket that would be her bed until they reached a township far enough away that she could let her guard down.

A blood curdling scream shook everyone awake and brought them to their feet within seconds. The sound of a horse struggling and then crying out in pain caused everyone to assume one of the horses had escaped or maybe a wolf got to it with their lookout unaware. They raised up their weapons and rushed to the tree where they'd tied their horses for the night. Lucky held up a torch he'd fashioned from the remnants of the fire to illuminate the scene and amid the orange glow the group saw horses that were spooked, but otherwise unharmed.

Morgan glanced apprehensively at the rest of the group. "Y'all heard that too. Right?"

As if in reply to his question, another hideous scream issued into the night, this time more primal and accompanied by a wet ripping sound.

Lucky turned around, torch first. "Maybe someone took their horse off the cliff and landed at the bottom of the ravine." He led the group back toward the jagged rock wall where the sound seemed to be coming from.

As they approached they saw a paint horse on its side writhing and kicking and a pale gaunt figure hunched over it. Lucky pulled back the hammer of his pistol with his thumb, making sure he did so loud enough for the shirtless figure to hear. "Turn around!" he ordered.

The shape lurched forward over the fallen horse one final time and turned around, while tearing a patch of flesh from the horse's throat with his broken teeth as he turned and snarled. A fist sized patch of hair had been torn away from the left side of his head and blood soaked his unkempt beard. This ghoul of a man growled, "Lucky," and lunged forward at the group with its jagged teeth bared and ready to tear apart whoever he reached first. Lucky fired a shot that connected with the creature's jawbone on its right side and turned the top right quarter of his skull into a red mist that stained the rocky wall provided by the ravine.

"What in God's name was that?" Joaquin asked.

"I don't think God had nothing to do with whatever it was." Lucky holstered his pistol and made eye contact with Morgan.

Morgan felt a sense of accusation coming from Lucky and asked, "Why are you looking at me like that?"

"Did you get a good look at that thing?" Lucky nodded down at the corpse. "If you weren't standing right in front of me, I'd've bet anything that it was you."

"What the hell are you talking about?" Morgan's voice held a blend of confusion and anger.

"He's right," Loretta spoke up. "That thing looked like you."

"That's bullshit!" He rasped back in a harsh whisper. "If you were so concerned with who that thing was, maybe you shouldn't have blown his head off, Lucky."

"One way to find out." Anton gave a resigned sigh and knelt over the body. He gently held what remained of its chin and turned its head revealing the half of the face that remained.

All eyes went from the body on the ground up to Morgan. They looked at him with a blend of sympathy, confusion, and fear. He stepped back and put his left hand up as if gesturing for them to stop. His right hand palmed the grip of his revolver.

"Why are y'all looking at me like that?" He took a step backward.

Anton stood up from where he still crouched over the body. "Morgan. Don't act like you don't see it. That's either you, or your twin brother, and you don't got one of those."

Morgan gave up on trying to keep quiet. "Listen. Don't stand there saying that's me. That ain't me! I'm standing right here."

"Does it got the scar from the time that sheriff's deputy winged you?" Lucky gestured to Morgan's right arm where a deep groove of scar tissue crossed the meat just above his elbow. At the time, Lucky thought it was fortunate that he got grazed there and not an inch or so lower. Back when he was fighting for the Union, Lucky had seen a man hit right about there and the bullet shattered the elbow. That man lost the arm. Now it seemed like the only way to confirm a fear they couldn't even articulate.

Anton stepped back from the body. "I ain't gonna be the one to look. Go on, Morgan."

Morgan stepped forward with such caution that one would think he half expected the body to rise up and come after him at any moment. He rolled the body to the side revealing the elbow. It had the same scar.

"That don't mean nothing!" Morgan recoiled from both the body and the group.

Lucky looked at him and at the ruin of a body on the ground. "I don't know what it means, but it ain't nothing."

"That ain't me. I'm standing right here! How can you say that's me?" Morgan shouted.

"That's not all," Loretta added. "Look at the horse. That's Joaquin's horse."

"Bullshit." Morgan argued, "Sure. It's a paint, but there's plenty of those. It ain't got no saddle. It's got to just be wild."

"I thought the same thing." Loretta looked sympathetic and fearful at the same time. "But it's got horseshoes."

Joaquin approached the dead horse and looked for any difference between it and the horse he'd ridden into this forest. The pattern of brown and white patches matched perfectly. As he continued examining the only difference he noticed were the wounds, one of which appeared to be from when a knife cut the strap of the saddle. Joaquin looked at the rest of the group. "I don't know how but...that's my horse."

"No," Morgan muttered. "I don't know if this is some kind of fever dream or what, but that ain't your horse and that sure as hell ain't me. I'm gonna take a piss, I'm gonna wake up from this dream, and we're gonna get out of here." Morgan walked away from the others and ducked behind a tree.

Before long, the rest of the group started to wonder about Morgan. Joaquin and Anton called out to him, at first joking about how long it takes for him to take a piss, but then with genuine concern. Lucky's gut told him that their bizarre experience may just be a hint of things to come so he called for the others to stay close as he checked behind the tree where Morgan had stepped a mere minute earlier. The remaining four circled the entire tree and saw no trace of Morgan.

"Morgan! Where are you?" Lucky called out, with less concern for stealth than he'd shown previously.

"Aren't you worried someone will hear us?" Loretta asked.

"Don't forget that gunshot. Anyone within a mile or two would have heard it," Lucky explained. "But I'm starting to think we've got bigger problems than a few farmers with hunting rifles."

Anton looked at the ground where Morgan had stepped behind the tree. "Nothing. No puddle of piss, no footprints trailing off, no sign that he was ever here behind the tree."

"Do you think he wanted to get away from that...thing?" Loretta grimaced and looked back at the corpse of some twisted version of

Morgan slumped next to the body of a partially eaten horse, both of which smelled truly ghastly.

"Sure, but not enough to walk out there alone." Lucky thought about what he knew of Morgan. "He certainly wouldn't have left without his share of the money."

"No way in hell," Anton agreed.

"I think it would be wise for us to stay together until we get out of this forest." Loretta suggested.

"Do you think something dragged him off?" Joaquin asked.

"I don't think anything, man or beast could drag Morgan off so fast he couldn't get a shot off, or at least holler for the rest of us," Lucky thought aloud.

There followed a long silence until Loretta had an idea. "Perhaps when we examined the body we were too focused on the similarities between it and Morgan. What differences are there between the two?"

"You mean besides half its face missing?" Joaquin scoffed.

"No, she's right," Lucky corrected. "There's a hell of a lot we don't know out here, and it wouldn't hurt to try to figure it out."

Anton examined the body closely. He didn't want anyone else to have to do it. He'd seen worse in his younger years, and Lucky had seen too much when he fought in the war. "This looks like Morgan alright, but it looks like he'd look if he hadn't eaten or bathed for a few weeks."

"That would explain him biting a chunk out of the horse," Lucky mused.

"He looks like he's been through hell," Anton continued. "There's a handful of hair that's been pulled out. He's covered in cuts and scrapes.

"Something happened to this Morgan that didn't happen to the one that went missing." Lucky knew that what he'd said was obvious, but he had to say it, if only to get the dark thoughts out of his own head.

"What are we supposed to do?" Loretta asked.

It was times like these that reminded Lucky why he always worked to get himself busted back to Private whenever his superiors back in the Union Army tried to promote him. For him, making decisions that would likely send someone he cared about to their death was worse than taking that chance himself. "Alright, y'all. We're going to stay here the rest of the night. Two of us on lookout, the other two sleeping.

Nobody gets out of anyone else's sight. Come sun up we'll look for Morgan and if we don't find him by noon, he's on his own and we're gonna get the hell out of these woods as fast as we can."

"We're going to leave Morgan behind?" Joaquin cocked an eyebrow doubtfully.

Lucky knew that it wasn't like him to suggest leaving a man behind, but he also felt like they were in way over their heads. "We're going to look for him, and on our way out, we can look for him too, but think about it. He hasn't been gone more than a minute. Certainly within hollering distance. We hollered and he didn't reply. Something ain't right."

"Maybe he's hurt and can't call out," Joaquin suggested.

Loretta said, "If he was hurt, we'd see him. It's not as if he could have fallen. We're at the bottom of the ravine." She wasn't sure if it was her place to be the arbiter of what the group should do, but she decided if she was going to start anew on her own, she'd need to be more assertive and she may as well start now. "The sun'll be up before long, and we can climb back up to the top of those cliffs and we'll be able to see the whole valley. Until then, it's best we get what rest we can."

Come morning, neither the sun nor their climb to the top of the ravine revealed where Morgan had gone. If he'd left them by choice, he must not have wanted to be found. What they did see was that there was a break in the trees about five miles to the northeast. That information coupled with the map Loretta kept of the area, and Lucky's compass, they knew that if they traveled upriver and crossed the river, they'd be in Dakota territory by sundown. By noon the following day they could be in Yankton, and from there Loretta and the men could go their separate ways and she could book passage to anywhere she wanted to from there. After the mind-bending encounter they'd had last night, the prospect of leaving it all behind seemed like such a simple task. Loretta had predicted difficulties, but not in the form of a horrifying double of one of their party attacking them in the night.

Now that Morgan was missing, but his horse wasn't, Loretta got her own horse, and after some halfhearted shouting of his name, the four of them headed toward the river, all the while making sure to stay within eyeshot of one another. The fact that Morgan went missing after only being out of their sight for a moment made them all uneasy, and despite any awkwardness that it caused, they made sure that if someone had to go off on their own to answer the call of nature, that at least part of their body remained visible at all times.

"We've been riding northeast for a while now. Shouldn't we have reached the river by now?" Loretta asked.

Anton looked down at the horses, measuring their pace and their gait. "We ought to be close by now at the very least. The terrain isn't too rough."

"Well...Hold on, then." Lucky raised his hand and waited for everyone to pause. "If we were close, wouldn't we hear the water?" He listened carefully and heard a light breeze move the upper branches of the trees with greenery so dark that it almost appeared black rather than green, but no water. Lucky glanced at the rest of the group and let his expression tell them what he hadn't heard.

"Perhaps we overestimated our pace," Loretta suggested, minding her tone to keep from sounding as if she'd accused Anton of being wrong. "Is it possible we already passed the river and merely didn't notice?"

They climbed from their horses and laid out Loretta's map and Lucky's compass. Lucky noted the direction on the compass and the position of the sun and noted that they were most certainly headed northeast.

Loretta traced her finger along the crooked blue line that marked where the river should have been. "Look at the path of the river. If we're anywhere in this area, there's no way to get to the other side of the river without crossing it."

"What if we ended up over this way?" Joaquin pointed to a point on the map far to the west where the river ran from north to south. "Then it would make sense that we hadn't hit the river yet."

"No. That ain't it." Lucky did his best to keep his tone even. "To get out that way, we'd have had to have ridden at least a few hours west out of Whisper Creek, and we sure as hell didn't do that."

Loretta's voice caught in her throat as she hesitated to give voice to what nagged at her mind. "What if it has something to do with what happened last night with Morgan?"

Lucky's forehead creased with the effort to understand. "How do you figure?"

She thought about how to say it without sounding crazy, but ultimately decided that it was more important to tell the others what she suspected and worry about how they'd react later. "Last night you shot Morgan, but Morgan was with us. Same with the horse. We still have that horse with us, even though we also saw it dead last night. It simply isn't possible, and yet it happened. It also isn't possible that we spent all morning riding northeast without reaching the river. Could it be that this forest doesn't take into account what's possible and what isn't?"

Lucky couldn't believe he was even considering something so preposterous, but he couldn't think of an alternative. "Say you're right. Then what do we do to get out of here?"

"If I'm right, then we can't even be certain where here is."

"Then that's what we need to figure out," Lucky decided. "I say we head up toward that rock formation, so we can get a lay of the land."

"That's at least a day's ride in the wrong direction!" Anton exclaimed. "I say we head back to the last overlook from this morning. It's back the way we came, but it's only a few hours ride away."

Lucky glanced at the rest of the group. "It's worth a try. It ain't like that other mountain is going anywhere." He sighed. "As far as we know."

They rode back the way they came until the sun hung high over their heads, and despite having just been there, the overlook never came. When the trail of their own horse's hoofprints suddenly stopped, even though the ground remained soft and pliable and would have left tracks that even a child could follow, Anton climbed down from his horse and looked more closely, as if to confirm what he'd seen from horseback. "Y'all. Our trail just stopped, and I don't see any sign of the overlook. Can any of y'all see the rock formation we were talking about before?"

"How is that possible?" Joaquin asked. "The ground is soft. The trail shouldn't just stop."

"I think Loretta was right. These woods ain't concerned with what's possible or what should or shouldn't be." Lucky's expression grew more grave. "I can't see the overlook anymore. I don't know how we're going to get out of here, but something tells me it might take a while. We're gonna start rationing our provisions until we figure out how to get out of here."

"Perhaps when we find a suitable place to make camp, we should take stock of what provisions we have," Loretta suggested.

Lucky nodded. "Until then we stay close. Anton, you keep your eyes open for any tracks that might be of use to use. Joaquin, keep an eye out for any high ground and once you see it, don't take your eyes off it for a second."

"I know I'm not one of your men, but we're in this together," Loretta spoke with more authority than she'd have been able to muster only a few weeks earlier. "What do you suggest I do as we travel?"

"Miss Loretta, you got this place figured better than the rest of us. I want the boys to keep their eyes open, but I want you to keep your mind open. You notice anything that might give us a clue as to what this place is or how we can get out, you let us know, and it don't matter how strange it sounds, because out here, strange is all we got."

Nearly an hour into their trek Loretta stopped the group. "I see tracks. I see our tracks."

Joaquin looked at the young woman with his exhaustion beginning to show. "We've followed our tracks before. Why don't we keep moving until we see something that might help."

"No," Loretta insisted. "This is important."

The group got down off their horses and examined the tracks. They were footprints rather than tracks left by their horses. Loretta lifted her skirts so she could kneel down without dirtying her clothing as she did so.

"We ain't been on foot other than to make camp," Lucky said.

"But that's exactly what makes this peculiar," Loretta explained. They're our tracks, three men, and one woman, even the same types of boots. What we need to think about is that there was never a time when we could have made them."

Anton knelt next to Loretta and investigated the tracks more closely, even touching them gently with the tips of his long fingers. "It gets worse."

"How's that?" Lucky asked.

"These tracks are a week old," Anton explained.

"But we ain't been here a week." Lucky protested.

"Maybe we have," Loretta mused. "Or we will."

Lucky digested the information fed to him by Loretta and Anton. "So if what you're saying is true, then by extension one might guess that the Morgan I shot was the same person, but after being lost alone in these woods for who knows how long?"

"It could have been weeks, maybe even months. His hair was longer, and he was so skinny. It looked like he hadn't eaten in…" Loretta's voice trailed off.

"Long enough that he'd try to eat a horse raw," Joaquin shuddered. "How is that possible?"

"I think it's best we stop thinking in terms of what's possible and what ain't," Lucky reminded Joaquin.

The group found a clearing and made camp well before the sunset. Normally, Lucky would've wanted to ride a few more hours before finding a place to make camp, but he thought it would be best for them to get a lay of the land before they let their collective guard down. Loretta had each of the men empty their packs onto a tablecloth she'd laid out and catalogued their supplies.

"One rifle, three pistols, plus my Derringer and ammunition for each of them. There's enough food for three days, five if we continue rationing. We've got saddles, horse blankets, canteens, flint and steel. We have my map, Lucky's compass, the clothing on our backs, and a lot of valuables that mean next to nothing out here." Loretta said, intentionally omitting the small knife that she kept on her person in case the men ever turned on her and took away her pistol. "We also have four horses, but that goes without saying."

Lucky committed the list to memory and did some quick mental math. "I know at least one of you is thinking it, so I'm just going to say it. It ain't a good idea to drop the valuables in order to cut down on the weight we got to carry."

"Why not?" Anton protested. "I'd rather get out of here a poor man than not get out of here at all."

"That ain't it." Lucky explained, "If we get out of here, I don't want there to be a single sane reason to ever come back to these woods. No tales of lost treasures, or hidden valuables. Once we're out, we don't look back."

"There's at least a few hours before sundown. What do we do until then?" Joaquin asked nobody in particular.

"We've learned a lot by observing our surroundings as we travel," Loretta offered. "Perhaps we can learn something useful by simply observing this strange land as we rest."

"That means, we set up camp. Joaquin, you make a fire. Anton, you see about fixing us some supper. Most important of all, nobody gets out of view of the rest of the group," Lucky ordered.

Loretta sat and tried to open her mind to her surroundings as much as she could and reminded herself that anything could be a clue to the mystery of this forest. She noticed a plump rabbit sniffing at the air at the edge of the clearing. In a hushed tone, Loretta told the group what she saw and when Lucky began to raise his rifle to shoot it so they could serve it for dinner, she silently halted him with a sharp hand gesture. "I want to observe it at the edge of the trees. We may notice something that could save our lives on our way out of this place."

She watched it sniff at the air and nibble at the leaves. It hopped forward into the clearing. Loretta asked the men to purposely take their eyes off of it for several minutes while she kept her gaze fixed upon it. The rabbit didn't disappear when she blinked or by simply being in the same place too long. Loretta waited until it slowly moved back toward the treeline one hop at a time. When it eventually stood between two thin trees, it hopped behind one and vanished behind it. Loretta called to the others. "The rabbit disappeared behind that tree."

"Which tree?" Lucky asked.

"That skinny one. It hopped behind it sideways, but it never came out the other side," Loretta explained. "Even though the tree isn't thick enough to block my view of the rabbit behind it, the creature still disappeared as if there were a doorway behind that tree."

"Maybe there is," Anton offered. "In a manner of speaking."

Loretta imagined Morgan disappearing the same way and her blood ran cold at the implications. "I think it would be wise to remain fully within sight of one another from now on."

Lucky shot a death stare at the two men, ensuring that they'd refrain from making any unseemly comments about keeping their eyes on Loretta, even when she is at her most vulnerable. Not only did Lucky consider himself to be a bit of a gentleman among thieves, he also had a daughter about Loretta's age and although he hadn't seen her or her mother in years, he knew he'd put a bullet in anyone who leered at her like a hungry wolf and he wouldn't lose an ounce of sleep over it.

Loretta watched falling leaves disappear behind the tree just like the rabbit did, and it remained that way for nearly an hour before they began to fall and actually land on the ground on the other side as they normally would. She noted that the doorways to other places and perhaps other times within the forest didn't stay in the same place. That would make them harder to avoid, should she or one of the others figure out a way to know where they were besides sitting around and hoping a small animal would happen by.

After they ate, Lucky stood up from the fire and announced. "Listen y'all. I know Miss Loretta here stared at that rabbit for some time on her own, and it didn't go nowhere until it went behind that tree, but just the same, we're going to have two of us sleep while two of us keep watch. The ones on guard will sit at opposite ends of the camp and watch each other with the sleeping two in the middle. If anything happens or if one of the two of you start to nod off, you holler and get the rest of us up as fast as you can. Got it?" Lucky didn't wait for them to agree. "Joaquin and I will take the first watch. Anton and Loretta take the second shift while we get some rest. Remember everyone. You fall asleep on the job, you might wake up alone in this God forsaken place."

The group made it through the night without incident, but Loretta silently wondered how long it would take for them to become exhausted and begin making careless mistakes. She prayed they'd find a way out of the forest before that happened. Loretta decided she wouldn't share her worries with the others. If they were to start volunteering to take watch more often, either to prove their own strength or force of will...that was another kind of stupidity that they simply couldn't afford.

Following the new rules they'd decided upon, the remaining four decided to travel northeast. Lucky acknowledged that direction didn't mean the same thing here as it did in the rest of the world, but they may as well pick a direction and stick to it until they had reason to go another way.

Four hours into the morning stretch of their trek, Loretta spoke up, her voice gravelly from a dry throat. "At least there's one thing that doesn't change when you take your eyes off it."

"What do you mean, Miss Loretta?" Anton asked, deciding that he'd believe whatever she said, so long as there seemed to be a reason behind it.

"From sunup until now, the sun has been positioned the way it ought to be, despite the fact that we obviously haven't been looking at it the whole time," she explained.

"Maybe it ain't the fact we haven't been looking at it," Lucky suggested. "Maybe we've been looking at the effects the position of the sun has on the land. We ain't been looking at the sun, but we've been seeing shadows and the like all morning."

"If the sun is where it belongs, then doesn't that mean north is still north out here?" Joaquin asked.

Loretta considered his question, and replied. "It's possible that you're right, and the true danger of the forest changing is after sunset."

"If that's the case, then we'd have to find a way out of here before the sun sets. After that we'd need to start over," Lucky mused.

"That's if our assumption is correct," Loretta said loud enough to make absolutely certain everyone heard, "we don't want to act like we've got this all figured out. The minute we do that, we'll miss some vital clues and end up like Morgan."

Loretta always made sure to remain at the back of the group. She had the idea that perhaps the person at the front of the line would be in danger of not keeping their eyes on someone and ending up turning around to find themselves alone. It was a strategic decision on her part not to share this information with the others. She tried not to hate herself for keeping what could be valuable information from the others, but Loretta was determined to make it out of this forest and start the new life she'd been planning. Joaquin rode at the front of the group, followed by Anton and then Lucky. Loretta watched him closely to see if her theory was correct.

The natural animal trail reached a bend, snaking around a narrow tree that bent to work its way around a large rock on the path. Joaquin turned the horse to follow the path and when she didn't see the nose of the horse appear from behind the tree like it would have anywhere else in the world, Loretta shouted for Joaquin to stop. By the time he got the horse to stop moving, its entire head had disappeared behind the tree from where Loretta and the others were.

"What's wrong?" Joaquin asked.

"Look at the front end of your horse." Lucky pointed, with his mouth hanging open in terrified awe.

Joaquin looked forward, more confused than worried. "What are you talking about?"

Loretta got down from her horse and held both hands out to Joaquin. "Just believe me when I say that you don't want to go past that tree." She waved him over. "Back up slowly, and get down from your horse."

Joaquin made eye contact with Lucky and immediately knew that he was in grave danger. He followed Loretta's directions to the letter, then asked. "What just happened?"

"Your horse went behind the tree, and she didn't come out the other end. It was like she just disappeared," Lucky explained. He got down from his horse, picked up the remnants of a branch about the length of his arm and cautiously stood just to the right of the tree. Lucky held up the stick to make certain that everyone had their eyes on it, then he threw the branch behind the tree, and nothing. Nobody saw it come out the other side. They didn't hear the sound of it landing in the brush. The branch was simply gone.

"You mean?" Joaquin started.

"That's right," Lucky confirmed. "If you took another couple steps, we wouldn't be talking to you now."

"Wait a minute," Anton interrupted. "I think I got something."

"What's that?" Lucky cocked an eyebrow.

"The horse went part way to...wherever the stick went," he explained. "But she came back."

"Are you proposing that anything that goes beyond a certain point, will have no way to return?" Loretta asked.

"Might be the case." Anton nodded.

Lucky furrowed his eyebrows, making his worn face show every ounce of its age. "Joaquin, how much rope do you have in your saddle bags?"

He produced a coil of rope from the saddle bags. "What do I tie it to?"

They decided that tying it to one of the horses was too great a risk. Instead, Joaquin tied it around the branch. Lucky fixed the other end to a tree, to ensure that they wouldn't lose the rope entirely. He tossed it beyond the tree, and while Joaquin saw it land with a mundane thump on the ground, the rest of the group neither saw it emerge from beyond the tree or heard it make any noise.

"Can you see where it landed?" Loretta asked.

"Of course," Joaquin replied. "And didn't you hear the loud knocking sound when it hit the rock?"

Before they could reply, a forceful pull on the rope sent Joaquin stumbling forward where he disappeared behind the tree. He fell forward and before they could get to him, the rest of the group only saw his left foot poking out from behind the tree. Lucky dove forward and grabbed Joaquin's ankle, making sure to stay clear of the tree that acted like a doorway to another time and place within the forest. When he looked up, he saw a haggard version of Morgan dragging Joaquin toward him on his belly. This time, the full extent of the ravages the forest had visited upon Morgan were fully visible in the daylight. A clump of hair had been torn out from the left side of his scalp, and his bloodshot right eye bulged from a fractured socket and stared straight ahead, regardless of where the left eye darted.

"Help me, y'all! Morgan's got him," Lucky shouted.

Anton and Loretta scrambled forward. They stood behind Lucky when they saw Morgan's scarred arms reach for Joaquin's belt.

"Get down!" Lucky let go of Joaquin and dove to the ground, shielding Loretta with his body.

Lucky rolled over and drew his pistol, but when he took aim, neither Morgan nor Joaquin remained. The only evidence of what had happened came in the form of a limp rope tied around a branch resting on the rocky ground. He kept his pistol aimed at the scene until Loretta stood up and slowly reeled in the rope. Then he asked, "What in the hell just happened?"

"Morgan must've been waiting there in another place, and another time to ambush us," Loretta said.

"How could he have been waiting in another time? He's been in these woods just as long as the rest of us." Anton scratched his head.

"Did you get a look at him, Anton?" Lucky brushed the dirt off of his shirt. "He looked like he hadn't had a shave in weeks. When he was with us, he had the makings of a beard, but what he had went down to his chest. He looked like he'd been through hell. If he weren't trying to kill us, I'd feel awful sorry for him."

"So you think–" Anton's voice trailed off.

"That's right." Lucky nodded somberly. "I expect he's been here a hell of a lot longer than we have."

There followed a long pause, as the three remaining members of the group came to terms with what they'd experienced. Their moment of introspection ended abruptly when the sound of a gunshot echoed off the valley walls. Loretta dove to the ground. Anton and Lucky raised their pistols, but remained standing.

"Not to worry Miss Loretta." Anton extended his hand to help her up. "That shot sounded like it was at least a mile away. Besides that, a bullet hits you before your ears have time to hear it, so it's best to try to figure out where it came from rather than try to dodge it."

"I bet that's Morgan, using the pistol he got from Joaquin to do some hunting." Lucky looked off in the direction of the shot. "Not the best tool for the job, but he looked like he was down to nothing."

"Will our provisions be enough?" The pace of Loretta's voice quickened as she imagined wearing away into both emaciation and madness like their former companion had.

"Wish I could tell you for sure," Lucky replied. "But it all depends on how long we're stuck out in these woods." He climbed back up onto his horse. "Come on, y'all. We either need to find our way out of here before dark, or we need to at least find a decent place to make camp for the night."

The three continued through the forest using the same method they'd used before the incident with Joaquin and Morgan. They managed to avoid the half dozen invisible portals to other times and places which Lucky had taken to calling doorways. When they finally made camp for the night, Loretta sat in silence for a long time.

"What's the matter?" Lucky asked. "Besides everything, I mean."

"I've been thinking about what happened with Joaquin," she sighed.

"There ain't nothing we could've done."

"That's not what I meant," Loretta protested. "It's tragic what happened to him, but I was trying to think of what we could learn from what happened."

Lucky took a knee beside her. "Did you figure something out?"

"I might have," she started. "But to be certain, we'll need one of the horses to take a terrible risk."

Lucky looked at the horses and then back at Loretta. "We got four horses and three riders. I suppose we could afford to take the risk if you think you could figure out something worthwhile. What have you got in mind?"

"We were able to retrieve the rope and the tree branch from the other side of the doorway, but not Joaquin," she explained. "Dead things."

"We might've been able to get Joaquin back if Morgan hadn't drawn his pistol on us," Lucky countered.

"That's precisely what I mean to test," Loretta continued. "We know we can pull dead things back. If we can do the same with one of the horses, then we might be able to keep from wandering through a doorway." A smirk stretched across her face and it felt foreign to her. "If we can do that, then it's just a matter of walking far enough in one direction and we get out of these damned woods."

Anton approached the two and stood over them. "How do we handle keeping watch now that there's three of us?"

"We need to have two people on watch at all times. Otherwise, it wouldn't take much for that person to turn around and see a completely new landscape before them." Loretta offered.

"Guess that means we're sleeping one at a time," Lucky grumbled and exchanged a worried glance with Anton.

"What is it?" Loretta asked.

"This place is wearing us down. We're gonna have less food, less sleep, less people. If we get too worn down, we're going to get careless."

Loretta did some mental math regarding their supplies and remaining sanity. "If this forest is testing our endurance, either on purpose or coincidentally, it's more important than ever that we find a way out as soon as possible. We need to test my theory with the horse first thing in the morning."

The sun crept over the horizon and Lucky, who volunteered to be the one to keep watch for two out of the three shifts, immediately got to work making a strong pot of coffee over their fire. He saw a reason to ration just about everything else, but they'd need to remain as alert as possible while they could.

Over their morning coffee the three finally took the time to ponder the reason behind their current troubles.

As she felt the hopelessness and desperation she'd been holding back push its way to the forefront of her mind, Loretta wanted to step away from her two remaining companions, but she didn't dare. Over the years, she'd seen many people fall victim to their own reactions to an insult or an injustice, often at the hands of her father and his men. Loretta had learned by the painful examples of others that taking the time to use her head instead of her heart as a guide was the best way to stay out of hopeless situations. She'd decided to live that way ever since she saw a man traveling through town die bloody in the street because one of her father's men had made a pass at the man's wife and he decided to fight to defend her honor. The man died, bleeding from a knife to his heart, and where did that leave the wife he died trying to defend? Alone, and without anyone to protect her. Still, Loretta had lived her life with cautious reservation and forward planning, and it led her to this place. To a forest in which the laws of nature, and of time abandoned their ways and instead operated in chaotic random ways. Part of her wanted to abandon her cautious calculation and fight chaos with chaos, but having seen what this place had done to Morgan, a man who had made a living by harnessing his ability to navigate lawlessness, she decided that allowing herself to lose her hard earned discipline would tear away the only tool she had.

"You alright, Miss Loretta?" Lucky asked.

"To be perfectly honest, Lucky. No." A single tear broke through Loretta's defenses and rolled down her cheek.

"I know what you mean." He sat down next to her. "I been in some tough scrapes over the years, even spent a night in a sheriff's cell expecting to hang the following morning. That's how I got the nickname Lucky."

Loretta brushed away her tears and then folded her arms as if she were trying to hide. "I didn't believe that talk about being related to the British nobility for a second. I always wondered why they called you that. How did you get away?"

"Truth be told, I shouldn't have. My crew got away from the job. I took a bullet in the leg and got dragged off to pay for all our crimes. The sheriff wasn't a bad guy, I've got to say. Sheriff Weaver was his name, and we were both much younger men back then. Lots of the lawmen I'd had run-ins with would've just let me bleed from the leg wound and let me hang in the morning if I didn't bleed to death. He brought in the town's doctor to patch me up, and he didn't say a single word of malice to me. If I were going to be caught by the law, I was glad it would've been him."

"What happened?"

"I never told nobody this. I sat in the cell alone, knowing damn well I wasn't going to sleep that night, knowing what awaited me in the morning. The time alone with my thoughts hurt more than getting shot in the leg ever did. After a few hours of trying to prepare my mind and my soul for what was to come, it might've been about three in the morning. I heard a voice. I knew it wasn't the sheriff. He'd left to go home to his wife. I saw a man, bearded and covered in dirt. He seemed to be there and not there at the same time. He looked like my daddy did when he'd come home from the mines back East. I asked who he was, and he told me he was a man who'd been hanged at the same gallows I was destined for, the difference was that he didn't deserve it and I did. When he told me he'd been hanged, I noticed the angle of his neck and I knew he wasn't lying. The man told me to tell his girl that he was okay in the great hereafter and told me to do some of the living he didn't get a chance to, then he left and came back with a key. He unlocked the cell and once I promised to deliver his message, he let me go." Lucky sighed. "I always figured that if I ever told anyone that story, folks would think I'd lost my mind. But after everything we've seen out in these woods...well, you and I both know that there's more to this world than most people realize."

"There are more things in heaven and Earth, Horatio, / Than are dreamt of in your philosophy," Loretta quoted.

"That's what I meant. Is that poetry or something?" Lucky asked.

"William Shakespeare wrote it. For better or worse, I suppose he was right." Loretta's eyes welled up with a whirlwind of both hope and fear. "Do you think the world will look different to us if we get out of here?"

"When we get out of here," Lucky corrected. "We've figured out a lot about this place thanks to you, and we're going to use that to find the best path out. Like you said. Let's go over the plan. You want to tie off a horse to try to figure something out. What about after that?"

Loretta wiped the tears from her eyes and let the facts of their situation and the plan to deal with it take the place of her worry. "We're going to use the horse to see if something alive can go into one of those doorways and come back. If they can, then Joaquin's horse is going to lead the way."

"Good. Then what?"

"Then we make our way through these woods, conserving our supplies and staying together until we find a place with a high overlook, and we're going to make camp there. The next morning, we're going to use the fact that the landscape doesn't change if you keep looking at it, and we're going to use the ropes and the remaining horses to march in a straight line as far as we need to in order to find our way out of this horrible place."

"That's right, and once we do, we ain't never coming back to these woods," Lucky confirmed.

It took them the better part of the day to find another doorway and they cautiously prepared Joaquin's horse for their experiment. Anton took off its saddle bags and anything else that could be useful to the group should they lose the horse within the next few minutes. Loretta briefly suggested that they attach some sort of message meant for Morgan to the horse, just in case he found it, but Lucky insisted that they all knew how Morgan would turn up in the forest.

"He and I both know that he's going to end up lunging to attack me and that I'm going to blow his head off. I know how Morgan thinks, insane or not. He's smart enough to know he can't save himself, but he'd be angry enough to want vengeance." Lucky's expression grew more grave.

Soon they sent Joaquin's horse forward with little more than a rope tied around it and they sent it into the doorway behind the tree. First, just the front half of its body which came back without incident. Then they had it step forward until all they could see was its tail, and it came back. Finally, they sent the entire horse through the doorway, the only lifeline being the length of rope tied around it. The moment the group lost sight of the horse, the rope fell limply on the ground and when Lucky and Anton reeled it in, there was no sign that it had ever been tethered to a horse.

"So much for tying ourselves in a line and just marching out of here," Lucky grumbled.

Loretta sighed, watching not only the horse, but also one of their hopes disappear. "The best we can do now is find a high vantage point and make camp there."

Several hours into the next leg of their trek through the woods, Anton stopped the group. "Do y'all smell that? Smoke."

Loretta let the acrid scent invade her nostrils, and she began to panic. "Is there a fire? Did someone try to burn down the forest?"

"I don't think so," Anton said. "I think it's a cookfire. Y'all stay close and we'll find out for sure."

Lucky and Loretta stayed close to Anton as he rode toward the source of the smell. The acrid smoke masked another smell, one that told each of them to run as they got closer to it, but if there was one thing they knew in the forest of uncertainty, it was that they couldn't break off from the group.

Anton turned beyond a particularly wide tree and froze when he saw what lay beyond. He turned back to the group.

"Is that meat cooking on a fire?" Loretta asked, her hunger more apparent than ever.

"In a manner of speaking, yeah," Anton stammered. "I don't know if you two ought to see what's burning over here."

"Maybe we ought not to, but we need to," Lucky decided. "We've picked up hints at how to get out of here from each of the horrors we've seen, and maybe we'll see something you missed."

They carefully maneuvered their horses alongside where Anton had climbed down from his horse and pulled his pistol from its holster. The fire had burned down to embers and the ruin of what had once been Joaquin's horse wrapped around it. The horse's hind legs were missing and its entrails dangled from its open abdomen into the fire where some of it still sizzled and other parts had become blackened and stiff.

"Is that the horse we lost only a few hours ago?" Loretta asked, examining the dappling rather than the hideous wounds the creature sustained before finally succumbing to them.

"Yes and no," Anton replied as he pulled his bandana over the lower half of his face and knelt closer to the creature. "Whoever took off its legs did so days apart. Look. They've both got stitches and the left one even started to scab over a bit."

"He tried to keep it alive while he cut off pieces when he got hungry enough," Lucky explained.

Loretta examined the surrounding area and saw the lengths of rope and wooden stakes driven into the ground used to pin the horse down while Morgan tortured the poor creature. "What made him finally stop?"

Lucky looked at the torn apart horse. "My guess is that the poor thing finally keeled over and died, so then he went for the organs before the meat could go rotten."

Lucky had seen many things in his long life, but he hoped that eventually he'd be able to close his eyes and not see the sight of the half cooked animal in his mind's eye. "Come on, y'all. We need to get the hell out of here and find some high ground. It ain't safe here."

As if confirming Lucky's sentiment, a shot rang out in the distance and a bullet tore a chunk of bark off the tree. Lucky grabbed Anton and Loretta by their shoulders and shoved them to the ground.

"He's shooting at us! We've got to get the hell out of here," Anton shouted.

"No. That's what he wants." Lucky pulled the two in more closely. "You know how good a shot Morgan is. If he wanted to kill us right now, he'd have been able to take at least one of us out. He's trying to force us to scatter, so we're lost on our own out here just like him."

The three kept close as they hurriedly escaped the trap that Morgan had laid for them. As they did so, a second shot rang out grazing Lucky's horse's shoulder. The horse reared up and broke into a gallop out of the area, nearly trampling Anton as it did so. Loretta led the way, swinging a five-foot length of rope in a wide arc in front of them. When the end of the rope wrapped around a thin tree and didn't appear on the other side, she shouted, "A doorway." and pulled the group around it. Suddenly, the three and their two remaining horses were in another part of the forest, devoid of the smell of gunpowder and burning meat.

Anton panted with the exertion of keeping their remaining two horses from running off. "Never would have thought that we'd actually seek out one of those damned doorways. Now where are we?"

"Another thing to ponder is when are we?" Lucky added. "I don't hear the shot echoing off the valley walls at all. Could be that from where we're standing, that shot was fired days, maybe even weeks ago."

"Or perhaps that shot hasn't been fired yet," Loretta guessed. "There's no way of knowing that. The only thing that matters is finding a high vantage point and getting out of here."

The first night, they made camp in the shelter of a fallen tree and by the light of their campfires, Loretta organized their remaining supplies. Since they'd lost a fifty foot length of rope, and half their food due to Lucky's horse taking off, she decided to split up their supplies evenly among bags that each of them would carry themselves. That way if they got separated, they wouldn't be stuck without any supplies. Thankfully, Lucky had his lever action rifle on his person when that shot sent his horse running. The majority of the ammunition for it was gone, but he still had what remained after shooting their way out of town and making their way into the woods.

"Lucky. How much ammunition do you have for your rifle?" she asked.

"Anton. Come here. I want you both to hear this." When they came close, Lucky continued, "I got seven shots left for the rifle. If I have to fire it, you keep count of the shots."

"Why?" Loretta asked.

"Because if he should fall and we have to take up his rifle, we'd need to know how many shots we have left." Anton answered.

"He's right," Lucky whispered gravely. "If things get bad, the last thing you want is to think that you have a loaded weapon when really you ought to be using it as a club."

Loretta nodded and then told them what supplies she was able to pack in each of their packs and told them her reason for splitting up the supplies the way she did.

"Good thinking, Loretta." Lucky patted her on the back. "Now you take first watch and then get some sleep. Anton and I will ge the second shift, and then you and I will take the last stretch before sunrise."

There followed three days of rain, dwindling supplies, and no sign of a decent vantage point to set up camp. Their only respite came in the form of having an easy means of filling their canteens and the fact that they hadn't encountered a single sign of Morgan that entire time. Growing accustomed to the methods of traveling through the woods and sleeping in shifts that allowed them to avoid the doorways and changes in the forest that had separated them from two of their group became second nature. Loretta continually reminded the men not to grow complacent or careless, which became harder for them to do with each passing day subsisting on minimal food and only a few hours of sleep each night.

On the fourth day, the rain stopped and when they happened upon a clearing, they decided to take an extended midday rest so they could make a fire and dry their clothes. Battered bodies and blistered feet would only feel worse if they spent any more time than necessary in damp clothing. Their stomachs growled and the fish from a stream they happened upon could only sustain them so much.

The following morning, the three came upon a high cliff overlooking the vastness of the strange forest. They climbed it and stood atop the rocky terrain and saw for the first time in what felt like forever, the world beyond the woods.

"We ought to make for the edge of the woods right now," Anton suggested.

Loretta gave him the same disapproving look that many of her tutors had given her over the years. "We haven't made it this far just to do something foolish now. If we keep our eyes on the horizon, and on each other, then it will still be there come sunrise. That's when we can make our way out of here."

Lucky knelt down on bended knee as if he were proposing marriage. "I say we make camp early, save our strength and get ready for tomorrow. That way we have the best shot out of here."

The day that followed had a sense of calm to it. Loretta wondered whether it was the light at the end of the tunnel, or the calm before a storm. She realized that if their plan didn't work, she'd have no clue what to try next, other than wander the forest aimlessly hoping that she wouldn't run into Morgan, or worse yet, end up like him. Loretta remained lost in her thoughts until Lucky got her attention. He moved slowly and spoke in a calm, but hushed tone. "Miss Loretta. There's a jackrabbit over by the brush." He gestured toward the last patch of scrubby bushes they'd passed climbing to the top of the cliff.

"Is there one of your doorways behind the bushes?" she asked.

"No. I think I can hit it with my rifle and we can get a decent meal before we try our luck getting out of here tomorrow." He explained. "Do you think I ought to?"

"You said that you have only seven shots remaining." Loretta didn't know whether that information would help him either way, but she did know it was accurate.

Lucky looked at the rifle. "That's right. If it were my last shot, I wouldn't try for it, but I think it might be a good idea to spend one to give us a shot at being well fed and thinking clearly tonight." He walked away and moments later a shot rang out with such ferocious volume that it sent a jolt through Loretta's body.

Within an hour, the group put together the meat and bones from the jackrabbit along with some morels and dandelion leaves that Anton found while scouting the area while keeping an eye on Lucky and Loretta. They put it all in their cast iron pot over the fire with their water and made a crude but nourishing soup out of it.

"It's funny how you don't realize how much strength a good meal gives you until you're really hungry." Anton thought aloud.

"Does that mean you're volunteering for the first watch?" Lucky chuckled.

"Does that mean you ain't up for it?" Anton countered.

Loretta looked down, hiding her amusement with the two men. She knew that if they got out of the forest, they'd go their separate ways, and likely never see one another again. She also knew that she'd never look back fondly on the days lost in these woods, but she'd remember Lucky and Anton as good men. Perhaps somewhat casual and crude in ways she wasn't used to, but with good hearts. Although she was educated to value etiquette highly, Loretta quickly realized that someone could follow every rule that society had invented and still have a heart black as coal and twice as hard. These men were the opposite of that, and she'd always remember them as such.

The three watched the sunset together and Loretta silently prayed that it would be her last sunset in these woods. She and Anton took the first watch while Lucky slept close enough to the fire to keep the chill in the air at bay. The night was so still that it almost appeared as if time were stopped on top of the cliffs. The wind didn't whistle and the branches didn't sway. Even the sky appeared to be a static image. The cloudless blanket of night illuminated their rocky camp with a dim blue light.

"Do you know anything about constellations?" Loretta asked. "I've read that people can navigate by using the position of the stars in the sky. They wouldn't even need a compass."

"I know a little about that." Anton shook his head. "But I don't think it would help us out here."

"Why not?"

"Nothing's where it ought to be up there. I see stars I ain't never seen before. There's constellations that aren't supposed to be in the sky during the same season sitting right there next to one another. Maybe that's us looking up at the sky in a dozen different times all at once, or maybe we're looking up at a different sky." Anton looked down at his own boots, escaping the enormity of the cosmos.

A rock the size of Loretta's fist bounced off the boulder they sat upon and rolled past them over the cliff's edge into the treetops below.

"What was that?" Anton drew his pistol.

"Should we wake up Lucky and tell him?" Loretta asked.

"Let's find out what to tell him before we do that," Anton suggested. "Get your pistol out, and if anything happens, holler loud enough to wake the dead."

Another stone dropped onto the rocky surface, this time smaller, more subtle, not much more than a pebble. Then another. Anton's eyes followed the path the pebbles took, but Loretta's gaze remained fixed on the direction from which they came. She looked and saw that the pebbles were coming from a dead tree, although calling it a tree might be giving it too much credit. To Loretta, it looked more like a branch that played at being a tree and failed miserably. Were the pebbles actually dried up berries finally falling from the husk of its source? A third pebble flew forward, more aggressively and Anton's eyes followed it so that he didn't see the gaunt, disheveled form of Morgan burst from behind the inch wide tree with a ferocious snarl.

Loretta dodged to the side and hollered just like Anton said she should. Morgan tackled Anton to the ground and clawed at him with the cracked bloody fingernails of his right hand while pinning down the hand that held Anton's pistol with his left.

"Lucky! Do I shoot him?" Loretta shouted as she held up the Derringer pistol.

"Don't shoot. You might hit Anton." Lucky reached for his rifle as he ran toward Morgan. "Remember. You've only got two shots."

With the speed reserved for animals rather than men, Morgan grabbed Anton by the shirt and rolled him over the cliff's edge, while tearing Anton's pistol from his grip as he fell. He turned and fired low. A red blossom of flesh and blood erupted from Lucky's thigh and he fell forward on top of the rifle.

Loretta raised up her pistol and fired a single shot that went wide over Morgan's shoulder as he charged her.

"It's your fault we got stuck out here!" he growled as he shoved her to the ground. "We'd've never come anywhere near these cursed fucking woods if you didn't want to rob your daddy and leave town. I'm going to take my time with you." He grabbed her by her hair and shoved her head into the rocky surface of the ground. The misplaced stars of the skyline swam around Loretta's vision and she pushed back at him ineffectually. She pounded her fists against his chest four times before she realized that she'd dropped her pistol.

Loretta reached out for anything she could use to get him off her, and she finally grabbed a fistful of hair on the right side of his head and pulled away a hideous mixture of hair, skin, and blood. As Morgan reared back in the blend of pain and rage that had consumed him ever since he saw his own body on the forest floor, Loretta used the fraction of a second she required to reach for her pistol and she shoved it forward, trying to make sure her final shot would find its mark.

As she readied herself to pull the trigger, Morgan lunged forward. Loretta wasn't sure if it was to bite at her or to avoid a bullet in his forehead. She squeezed the trigger and the bone structure of his right eye socket blasted away, leaving Morgan's eye permanently bloodshot and bulging from his skull just enough to make the eyeball look larger than it ought to be, and it stared straight forward at her.

Morgan released his grip on Loretta to raise a hand to reach up and touch his ruined face. As he arched his back away from her, Lucky snuck up behind him and dragged him backwards by choking him with the length of his rifle and pulling him back to simultaneously choke him and get him off Loretta.

"I'm going to get you, Lucky!" Morgan growled through being choked.

"No," Lucky countered. "We both know you ain't." He pulled Morgan sideways and tossed him over the edge of the cliff.

Lucky limped forward to see where Morgan landed. Instead, he saw Anton clinging to a root that had grown through the soil the rocky cliff sat upon. "Shit, Anton. They ought to call you Lucky instead of me."

"Call me whatever you want, just help me up!" he shouted back.

Loretta and Lucky hoisted Anton back up to the relative safety of the cliff's edge before Loretta and Anton noticed the bullet wound in Lucky's thigh.

Anton tore the sleeve off his shirt and fashioned a crude bandage that at least slowed down the bleeding. Loretta asked if they needed to remove the bullet from his leg, but Lucky explained that the bullet had done enough damage on the way in, and if anyone but a doctor tried to take it out, they'd do more harm than good. By the time they'd patched Lucky up and helped him sit down in a comfortable position, the subtle glow of the oncoming sunrise turned the horizon red.

"Come on, Lucky. We've got to get you up onto a horse if we're going to make it out of here," Anton said.

"Anton. We both know that if you two stand a chance of getting out of here, I can't be with you to slow you down."

"No!" Loretta protested. "We can put you up on one of the horses."

"You could," Lucky started. "But it'd take half the day to get me down these cliffs in one piece. Besides, there's one thing I thought of that you might not have."

"No," Loretta repeated, this time a whimper.

"Those woods will move the second someone takes their eyes off them. Same goes for the edge of the woods on the horizon." He sighed. "The only way to be sure that the forest's edge stays put is if someone stays up here and keeps an eye on it. I'll just sit here a spell and do just that while you two make a break for it."

"You're sure?" Anton broke eye contact after only a few seconds, since he knew any more would break him as well.

"I'm sure. Now go get anything we got left worth having and pack it onto those horses."

"Lucky, I don't give a damn what you say. We're not leaving you without one of the horses." Loretta's voice left no room for anyone to protest.

"That's real kind of you, Miss Loretta." Lucky waited for Anton to go start packing up their supplies. "I got hit in the same exact spot where

I got shot all those years back. What are the odds of that? Hell. Maybe it's fate. Maybe it's more than just luck. I figure if it's possible for a place like this to exist, then it's possible that I was meant to live long enough to help you two get out of here. If that's the case, then I suppose the great hereafter is coming to collect."

"Don't talk like that." Loretta wiped tears from her eyes. "We'll come back for you."

Lucky's nostalgic expression grew more grave. "Miss Loretta. I need you to promise me that you won't. Don't ever come back into these woods. Promise me, and I'll know if you're lying." He patted his rifle. "If I so much as think you two will come back here for me, I'll put a bullet in my head without thinking twice about it."

Loretta steeled herself. "I promise we won't come back. But you've got to promise me something."

"Anything for you, Miss Loretta."

"Promise me that you won't quit. You sit here and watch the horizon until nightfall, but after that, I want you to get on that horse and ride until you can't ride anymore."

"I promise." Lucky straightened his hat on his head. "Now you and Anton get out of here. You've got until nightfall to reach the forest's edge. Hurry, but don't do nothing stupid on your way out."

As Loretta and Anton walked the horse down the precarious path facing the horizon, Lucky climbed onto his horse for a better vantage point and kept his gaze fixed upon his two friends and the horizon. He didn't move or avert his eyes even when Loretta and Anton were little more than specks in the woods and the sun began to set at his back. Lucky whispered a silent prayer that his friends made it out and thought about the years since he'd earned his nickname. He realized that it fit better than he ever thought it did. He may have been living on borrowed time and living dangerously, but he'd met some good folk along the way and if the last thing he ever did on this earth was help Anton and Loretta get back into the world where they could lead lives of their own, it was well worth it.

Loretta and Anton stepped through the final row of trees on the forest's edge and when they saw the dirt road they ran for it as if it could slip away from them if they blinked. They dropped to their knees in the road and fell into a tearful embrace that lasted for several minutes before either of them could form words.

"Thank you, Anton." Loretta exhaled with relief.

"No, Miss Loretta. You were the one who noticed little things that helped us figure out how to get out of there. I ought to be thanking you."

"We each did our part." Loretta wiped away her tears. "Where will you go now?"

"I got people out California way," Anton explained. "I wasn't planning on going out that way to meet them any time soon, but after everything we've been through, maybe it's time."

Loretta shook his hand. "I wish you well, Anton. Take the horse and go. If people find us looking like this," She gestured down to her dirty and disheveled dress. "They'll likely assume y'all took me hostage."

Anton knew she was right. He climbed up onto the horse and turned to look back at Loretta one last time. "I hope you find the life you were looking for, Miss Loretta." He rode west, and didn't stop until he disappeared over the horizon.

Loretta began the long walk towards Sioux City. It would take her a long time unless someone happened by and offered to escort her into town, but she was determined never to return to Whisper Creek, Nebraska and she supposed that her best chance at that would be to make it to Sioux City where she could book passage on a train.

She walked through the night, and although her feet ached she at least felt certain that the road would still be there if she took her eyes off it for a moment. When it got too dark to see where she was going, she found a soft patch of grass on the side of the road and slept, using the spare set of saddlebags that Anton left behind as pillows.

She woke in the morning to a horrible sound that sounded like the honk of some large and monstrous duck. When she opened her eyes she saw a rectangular machine that looked like something between the engine of a train and a horse drawn carriage, except there weren't any horses pulling it. A man in a suit with slicked back dark hair stepped out from the machine. "Excuse me, Miss. Do you need help?"

"What is that thing?" Loretta couldn't help but ask.

"Are you quite alright? It's an automobile. It's a newer one, the latest Packard Twin Six Roadster. Just came out in the spring of 1926. Haven't you seen one before?" The man stepped closer cautiously, trying not to let his confusion overshadow his concern for the wellbeing of the young woman.

Loretta tried to mask her astonishment. "Of course. I apologize. I'm a bit out of sorts. Did you say 1926?"

"Of course. Ma'am, can I drive you to a hospital? I hate to sound rude, but you look like you've been injured."

Loretta's mind reeled. She entered the woods in 1892 and although it was only a few days from her perspective, apparently at least thirty-four years had passed. She tried not to show the maddening mixture of relief and horror at the thought that when she left to start a new life, she'd done more than that. Anyone who might've been looking for her had either died or given up in the decades she'd been gone. "I was lost in the forest for...several days. Perhaps I should see a doctor."

The vehicle moved faster than a horse ever did, and it made Loretta nauseous. The man slowed the machine down when she expressed that she was beginning to feel sick to her stomach. The doctor determined that there was nothing physically wrong with Loretta, other than mild dehydration and that she could be released shortly. Loretta made sure not to tell anyone where she'd been or when she came since she was certain that they'd assume she'd gone mad and lock her away somewhere. She decided that she'd simply have to acclimate to her new situation on her own, and while she quickly got used to wearing dresses that were shorter, and in her opinion more comfortable, other things would take longer. She'd survived one story and would survive many more before finding the life she'd wanted.

Rather than San Francisco or New Orleans, she traveled to Boston where she found a comfortable life and married a young man named Alexander, who had fought in something called The Great War which she'd apparently been lost in the woods for the duration of. The two bought a small apartment building in Boston and lived in it for some time with their tenants until Loretta found herself with child and they decided to move to Franklin, Massachusetts for a more peaceful life outside the city.

At first, Loretta thought about her time lost in the woods with Lucky and the others often. As she got older and her new life got busier and more removed from her old one, she thought about them only on very still nights when the sky seemed to be frozen in place. On one such night, many decades after her escape from the forest, she was out in Boston celebrating her husband's retirement. When she sat back down after a champagne toast, she noticed an older man sipping whiskey slowly at the bar. He turned and she could have sworn that it was the same thoughtful but mischievous smile Lucky would often wear even when their time in the forest became quite dire.

They made eye contact and he raised his glass before downing the remainder of his drink and walking off in a very well appointed suit with a woman with red hair on his left arm and an ornate wooden cane in his right hand, aiding the slight limp he had.

Loretta tried to catch up to him before he left, but as she got outside of the restaurant, the man and the woman he was with had gotten into a chauffeured car that took off heading west out of Boston. She liked to think that it was him, although she knew the odds of someone getting out of that forest on their own. Still, they called him Lucky for a reason.

Acknowledgements

I'd like to start these by acknowledging the artists who contributed to this collection. I appreciate your efforts and admire your talents. Seeing my words come to life in the form of visual art fills me with awe and their ability to do that is something I will always admire.

A huge thanks also goes out to the readers who took a look at these stories as I was working on them. Your suggestions and other commentary were very helpful and valuable. These readers include Alexia Merkouriou, Nancy Manning, and Marc Bilodeau.

Finally, I'd like to thank the HOWL Society for being a constant source of inspiration, entertainment, and thoughtful commentary. Their contributions to the horror genre are truly incredible.

.